KADE HOLLEY
Forest Ranger

By Dan Kincaid

ISBN 13:978-1548026981

ISBN 10:1548026980

Published by: Kade Holley Publishing and Create Space

Editing: Kade Holley and Sydney Lough

Cover Design: Shannon Lough and Kade Holley
Publishing

Cover Art and Illustrations: Mary Linscheid

Printed in the United States of America.

TABLE OF CONTENTS

INTRODUCTION

Kade Holley is a fictional Forest Ranger with the U.S. Forest Service. Throughout this book, and hopefully future books, he gets involved with numerous adventures in the course of his work. Kade loves his job, working at various National Forest locations in his career. He understands that his work is sometimes dangerous, often challenging, and always fun and interesting. That's life as a "ranger."

I've chosen to call Kade Holley a Forest Ranger because it is the title that most of the public associates with this career. Actual job titles for foresters with the U.S. Forest Service can vary somewhat, but include Forester, District Ranger, Assistant Ranger, Forest Supervisor, and others.

Kade works for the U.S. Forest Service, an agency within the U.S. Department of Agriculture. It is a separate agency from the National Park Service, which is part of the U.S. Department of Interior. Many of the Park Service employees are referred to as Rangers, perhaps even more so than Forest Service employees. It can get a little confusing, but for purposes of my book, Kade Holley is a Forest Ranger or "Ranger" working at various National Forest locations.

DEDICATION

With love to Vicki, my wife and best friend; together we have shared an amazing 46-year journey.

REVIEWS AND READER COMMENTS

Dan's book brings to life a range of situations and emotions that forest rangers must deal with in their day to day work. I appreciate *Kade Holley's* adventurous spirit and deep love for nature, as well as his dedication to doing his job well. I hope this book inspires a new generation to pursue a career in forestry or other natural resource fields.
Jason Reed, Athens District Ranger, Wayne National Forest, Ohio

I have been fortunate to work with Dan Kincaid on several occasions during my career. In his book, *Kade Holley – Forest Ranger,* Dan has drawn from his experiences with the U.S. Forest Service to create a series of exciting adventures. These will appeal to anyone, particularly the young reader, who loves the great outdoors; who enjoys exploring our country's many state and national forests; and who dreams of a career in forestry.
Erin Albury, Field Operations Chief, Florida Forest Service

As a gifted storyteller, Dan brings together a wealth of knowledge and experience that will fascinate young readers and enlighten anyone interested in natural resource management. By using vivid and exciting accounts of real work experiences, he conveys insight into the challenges that a *"ranger"* faces and why it can be an attractive and rewarding career.
Don Girton, Retired, USDA Forest Service

As stated above, Kade Holley is a fictional person. His adventures in this book, as well as other characters, are fictional. I have chosen locations for Kade's adventures to occur on National Forests where I worked in my 31-year career with the U.S. Forest Service. This allows me to lend a more accurate and realistic feel for the stories that I create.

For those readers contemplating a career as a forester or forest ranger or any other related outdoor profession, I sincerely hope that Kade's adventures will inspire you to pursue your dreams.

Read on and enjoy the adventures of .... *Kade Holley, Forest Ranger*.

- *Dan Kincaid*

Chapter 1

Boundary Waters Plane Crash

As the engine made a final sputter, the pilot banked hard left to put the plane on a steep glide path toward the only lake close enough on which to land. Despite this being such a small lake, the chance to survive was still much greater than crash landing into the thick spruce forest directly ahead.

Had Kade's luck finally run out?

A few short hours earlier Kade Holley and Paul Brown had been making final plans and readying their gear for a three-day work trip into the Boundary Waters Canoe Area. They were employees of the Superior National Forest in northern Minnesota, not far from the Canadian border. Every month they took a similar trip. They would review work progress of their portage and trail maintenance crews. They would take notes on future work assignments for their crews. And they would look at various sites to discuss plans for long-range projects.

It may have seemed like nothing but a fun job to most observers, but it was hard work with long hours. It required serious thought and considerable experience, too. You couldn't just pull someone off of a city street corner to do this type of work. Kade had a bachelor's degree in forestry and most of the technicians had two-year degrees. In addition, of course, their on-the-job experience was extremely important, but so was the educational background.

Kade often thought that his career with the U.S. Forest Service sure beat working in a factory or steel mill in Cleveland or Pittsburgh, or being a coal miner in his native state of West Virginia. But still, it was a difficult and sometimes dangerous job. No doubt about that.

Kade had selected a canoe from the District's storage yard and was busy lashing it to the overhead rack of his pickup truck. He had also picked up two portable radios and plenty of extra batteries to take along. Communications with home base was very important, and sometimes even a matter of life and death.

Paul, whom everyone called PB, was always in charge of the food and Kade had to admit that he did a great job.

They never ran out of anything and it was usually pretty tasty, too - even the freeze-dried items. Plus, Paul always planned a surprise meal for one evening.

Of course, they each packed their own personal items and clothing, as well as the required work items – notebooks, pencils, pens, maps, aerial photos, a compass, knife, first aid kit, and numerous other necessities.

No guns though. Not anymore. The Forest Supervisor had put a stop to that after one of the former rangers had been caught by the local Game Warden shooting bears at the campsites. Even though the bears were a danger to the campers in the area, you still had rules to follow and laws to obey. You couldn't just shoot them. Kade knew that and had agreed with the hefty fine and the firing of Billy Bagwell.

Billy had claimed that he was just trying to make things safer for the public, yet all of the forest rangers knew there were proper ways to go about handling the bear problems. State wildlife officials could trap them, issue special hunter permits to kill problem bears, or if all else failed they would kill the bears themselves.

But still, Kade had mixed feelings about the gun ban. It sure felt good to know you had a firearm with you, just in case you ran into certain situations. This area was, after all, one of the more remote and wild areas in the lower 48 states. There were black bears, lots of them, as well as moose, wolves, and, yes, more than a few odd characters that you would run into from time to time.

On this trip Kade and PB wouldn't need a tent. They would base their day trips from the cabin on Conkle Lake. It was one of two cabins located on the District, built back in the 1930's by the Civilian Conservation Corps. They were used for administrative purposes only, although many of the locals knew where the cabins were located, and could get to them in case of an emergency while on a fishing or hunting trip.

Kade looked forward to the cabin trips. Sleeping in a tent wasn't as much fun as it was when he was a teenager. And there was more chance of an encounter with a rogue bear when you were tent camping. In the cabin, you were sheltered from rain; there were beds, tables, chairs; and you could throw a log into the fireplace if you needed a little warmth. Kade would take a cabin over a tent any time.

Wolves had never been a problem for any of the District employees, although there were always the stories, never documented, of being followed by a pack of wolves. Kade had to admit that it did make you wonder sometimes though. The howling, yipping, and yapping that they often heard gave you an eerie feeling at times.

A pack of wolves, even a small pack, was definitely known to bring down an adult deer and an occasional moose. Still, Kade never worried about wolves. Truth is, you seldom saw one, even though you knew there were plenty of them in the area.

Occasionally a moose with young ones, or a bull moose during mating season, would charge at one of the foresters. One of the employees on the adjacent District had been forced to shimmy up a tree last year when a moose stomped and charged at him. He had remained in the tree for over an hour, standing on a limb and holding on for dear life, before the moose finally gave up and left.

Usually the bears ran away when they saw you. Only occasionally would a female bear with cubs get nasty. Kade could attest to that. He, too, had been chased up a tree two years ago by a black bear; and even more frightening, it began climbing the tree after him. He kicked at it several times and was nearly pulled from the tree as it angrily clawed at his boot. Only after he was able to toss his field vest onto the bear's head did it jump down from the tree and run into the nearby brush. Kade, too, had stayed in the tree for over an hour, making sure the bear was gone, before he came down. The bear had ripped the vest to shreds, making Kade shudder at the thought of what had almost happened.

Bears, wolves, and moose were interesting to talk about, but the truth was that bad weather and accidents were the real worries. Being caught out on a lake during a cold rain, with heavy winds and lightning, was extremely dangerous. Kade had experienced that a couple of times. Although he hadn't actually feared for his life in either case, he had to admit later that he probably should have. Normally, Kade and PB could plan their trips around predicted bad weather. But weather forecasts were not guaranteed. Like a former boss had once jokingly remarked, "Prediction is a difficult art, especially when it involves the future." Wasn't that the truth, Kade thought?

Accidents, although always a possibility, were not common for the forestry employees. In Kade's time working at this national forest, he could remember only three major incidents, and these had all occurred on adjacent Ranger Districts – one employee had received a severe head wound from a fall along a boulder-strewn lakeshore over close to Grand Marais; there was one near case of hypothermia, when a crew tipped over a canoe several miles from their campsite on Knife Lake; and last summer near Isabella, Jerry Hines had caught his foot on a root, twisted it while falling over a small log, and ended up with torn ligaments in his knee and an ankle broken in three places. Even with extensive rehab Jerry still walked with a limp and, according to his doctors, would likely never recover fully. In all three cases, though, the agency's Beaver aircraft had flown in to evacuate the employees to the local hospital in a timely manner before the incidents turned into life threatening situations.

By the time Kade had finished securing the canoe to the truck rack, loading his gear, two extra paddles, and throwing in a few tools, PB had returned with the food and all of his gear. One of the long-time assistant rangers, Joe Lakitch, arrived to drive Kade and PB to the float plane base, which was about five miles away.

The flight to Conkle Lake would take only about 25 minutes if they flew directly there, but Kade had asked the pilot, Deke Ballman, to make a pass over the Cadillac Mountain Trail on their way. This would take an extra 20 minutes or so, but Kade wanted to see how much damage had occurred from last night's July windstorm that had blown through the area around midnight. Reports were that the winds were heaviest just northeast of town and out toward Cadillac Mountain. The trees in that area were older than in most other parts of the District and it seemed like every time a big wind storm came through, there were fallen trees and a lot of trail clearing to do.

Deke was at the dock, going through pre-flight checks, when Joe pulled up to the base. He backed out as close as he could get to the plane, and they unloaded their gear and the canoe. They lashed the canoe to one of the plane's floats, loaded their gear behind the cargo net, signed a few forms, and made plans for Joe to pick them up at the dock on Friday at noon.

Deke was a great pilot, as were all four pilots who worked at the forest. Deke, Monty, and Stan flew mostly from the lake – on floats, as long as the lake was not frozen, and on skis after that. Conrad did quite a bit of that, too, but he also flew wheeled planes from the airport about 10 miles from the float plane base. It was an adventure working at a Ranger District with this much plane activity. No other eastern or southern National Forest had this; you would have to work at one of the western National Forests for such an experience as the Superior National Forest afforded.

Monty Montgomery had been an Air Force pilot. Stan Wellman had grown up flying in this area and he knew it like the back of his hand. He had logged his first solo flight before he was old enough to drive a car. Conrad Juskila had been a light aircraft instructor pilot downstate before moving north several years ago.

But Kade's favorite was Deke, who had graduated from the local high school before joining the Army. When he was discharged a few years later, he went to Alaska with an Army buddy and he stayed there for 20 years. In the process he got married, learned to fly, raised a girl and boy, and became one of the best bush pilots in a state full of good bush pilots. When Deke's father passed away, he and his wife decided to move back to Deke's hometown and care for his mother. That had been five years earlier. The Forest Service was lucky indeed to get a pilot of Deke's caliber to fill a vacancy that had been created due to a retirement.

PB crawled into the back seat and Kade sat in the co-pilot's seat, as he normally did. Kade, after all, had a private pilot's license, although he hadn't flown much in recent years. He had obtained his license while in graduate school in North Carolina years ago. His experience was primarily flying in a Piper Cherokee and a few times in a single engine Cessna. He had never taken off or landed a float plane. Still, he knew he could take over the plane if something happened to the pilot.

All three men strapped in and Deke throttled the Beaver forward to taxi out onto the lake in preparation for takeoff. Just another day at the office, Kade thought, as Deke gave it full power and headed straight down the lake, bumping against the water as he gained enough speed to lift off.

Kade knew that not much could go wrong on these flights except during takeoffs and landings. And once they had cleared the takeoff pattern, gained some altitude, and were headed toward Cadillac Mountain, it should be an uneventful 15 minutes or so until they could check out the trail area for trees blown down or damaged by the windstorm.

This part of the District was a little different from the rest. There weren't as many lakes on the east side of the forest and Kade thought the miles of trees were beautiful to see from the air. Another five minutes and they could start checking out the hiking trail. Kade knew exactly where it came into his District just below the rocky peak of Cadillac Mountain.

It wasn't really much of a mountain, Kade had always thought, compared to those back home in West Virginia. But it was the highest point in this part of the forest. The forests of the Lake States were mostly flat, unlike the steep terrain in his Mountain State home. Often, on these flights over northern Minnesota, Kade would daydream about West Virginia.

Suddenly, a severe vibration jolted the plane and Kade saw Deke going through all kinds of checks to determine what had happened. The plane seemed to be losing power and airspeed. The engine began to miss and sputter, as Deke continued to try everything he could to figure out what was going on.

Kade tried to hold his emotions in check, but he was

very concerned. No, check that, he thought, as he felt his heart rate soar. He was more than concerned; he was downright worried. It seemed to him that they would have to crash into the woods. No way could they land on that rocky mountain peak straight ahead, Kade thought.

Just then, the plane made a final loud sputter and the propeller stopped. This was a fine time to be flying in a single-engine airplane, thought Kade, as he looked over his shoulder to check on PB, whose face was as white as a sheet. No sooner had Deke told them both to tighten their lap and shoulder straps, than he banked the plane sharply to the left.

Kade had no idea what Deke was doing. These Beavers could glide quite a distance, if they were at higher altitudes. That wasn't the case this time, however, because Deke had been flying a little lower than normal to be able to see the Cadillac Mountain Trail.

As Deke brought the plane out of the tight bank and made a "mayday" radio call to home base, Kade could tell that they had lost considerable altitude. Deke had the nose of the plane pointed down to maintain airspeed and keep it from stalling. If it stalled, the Beaver would fall like a rock. Kade knew there was a better chance for survival if they flew into the woods with wings level, rather than stalling and falling from the sky.

Finally, Kade understood Deke's plan. He was headed on a steep, straight glide path to the only nearby lake, one that Kade had almost forgotten about – Lone Tree Lake. It was a small lake that was located off by itself and not part of any of the normal canoe routes on the District. Once in awhile a few people hiked into Lone Tree from the Cadillac Trail to fish, but that was about it. Kade had never known a float plane to land there because it was too small, but it appeared that was what Deke was trying to do.

Kade guessed that they would have a better chance to make it out of this situation if they could make it to the lake instead of having to crash into the forest. But from the look of things, he wasn't sure they could make it that far. The ground seemed to be rapidly gaining on them. At the rate they were losing altitude, it was going to be a toss-up as to whether or not they could make it over the tall pines growing along the lakeshore. What a mess, Kade thought.

His thoughts drifted to his wife, their daughter, and two sons. He sure wished he could tell them how much he loved them again. There were many things he still hoped he could do with them. But now, was this the end?

What seemed like hours actually took less than a minute; and it now began to look like they might possibly make it to the lake. However, whether or not they would clear the pines along the shore was definitely in doubt. Deke lined up the plane to glide over the shortest tree he could spot and he held the wings steady.

Whoosh! The left pontoon smashed against the top of the shorter pine about the same time that the right wing hit the limbs on an adjacent tree. The plane shook violently and Kade thought his luck had finally run out. He just knew that this was the end. Even if the plane reached the water, they'd probably all drown.

How Deke maintained control of the aircraft and kept the wings level, as it glided toward the water, was anyone's guess. But he did and it barely crossed the water's edge before it stalled and dropped the last several feet into the water. The impact threw each man harshly against his straps, but with a quick look around, it appeared to Kade that all three had made it through the rough landing.

The plane was still afloat, although it tilted substantially toward the damaged pontoon with the left wing almost touching the water. They were not more than 50 feet from the shore and it seemed that a quick exit of the craft was the sensible thing to do. Deke made a quick radio call and reported the situation to base station. PB grabbed a portable radio and the backpack full of food. No telling how long they would be here before help came. Kade unlashed the canoe from the right pontoon in record time and soon all three men were in the canoe with Kade paddling them toward shore.

It was a few minutes before 11:00 a.m., Kade noticed, as he guided the canoe just to the left of a large bolder at the edge of the lake. It was flat and shallow on that side and made a perfect place to beach the canoe. Not one of them had said a word in the last several minutes. Knowing PB and Deke like he did, he figured they were busy saying a prayer of thanks for what had just happened.

They weren't through the ordeal yet, Kade knew, but survival was almost assured. A check with Deke revealed a deep cut just above his left ear, but the bleeding had already stopped. Later on at the hospital, after they had returned to town, Deke would receive six stitches, so the wound would heal better. PB had two sore wrists where he had braced himself against the back of the seat in front of him. He later found out that he had a hairline fracture in his left wrist. Kade had suffered a severe sprain to his right knee. An MRI the next day would reveal no major damage, although it took several weeks before his knee was back to 100 percent use.

In less than half an hour another Beaver aircraft was circling above them with Stan at the controls and Joe in the passenger seat. As Kade made radio contact with them, all three men waved to the plane indicating that they were okay. Though none of their injuries seemed to be life threatening, Stan suggested, and Kade readily agreed, that requesting a Coast Guard rescue chopper from the Lake Superior Station would be a wise move.

The chopper could be there in about an hour, lift them out, and have them back to town by early afternoon.

A ground rescue would mean coming out by land over the Cadillac Mountain Trail. Even without their injuries, that would be difficult and time consuming. They might not even make it back before dark. And, of course, landing another Beaver on Lone Tree Lake was out of the question.

For now, they were content to wait for the Coast Guard helicopter, eat a bite, and contemplate what might have been. This was probably the closest call that Kade or PB had ever had, although they both had been caught on lakes in lightning storms; had encountered bears and moose; and had tipped over canoes in precarious situations. Deke told them that he had been in three or four worse situations while flying in Alaska, although Kade didn't see how that could be true. Still, it gave him and PB some level of comfort knowing that Deke had been there before, so to speak, although every situation was a little different. Yes, Kade thought, Deke was still his favorite.

Half of the ditched Beaver was now under water and it had blown a little closer to shore. Deke's main worry seemed to be how they would ever get his favorite aircraft back to base and whether or not it could be salvaged to fly again. This, however, was not something Kade cared about at the moment; in fact, it was the last thing on his mind.

Kade was thinking about his wife and three kids, how lucky he was to have them, and how great it would be to see them all in a few hours. He was thinking about his life as a forest ranger. He really enjoyed it, danger and all. He couldn't think of anything else he would rather do. And he was thinking that this would be another story to one day tell his grandchildren: How Kade Holley had once cheated death and crash landed in a float plane in northern Minnesota on a lake so small you could barely see it from the air.

Chapter 2

Incident at Ray's Run

Six guys to our two, Kade thought, as he slowed down to take a quick look at the vehicles parked in front of the gate to Ray's Run Natural Area. Several years ago the Forest Service had designated it as a "walk-in only" area and installed the gate. Some local people didn't like that because the old township road had always been open. Even today with a jeep or four-wheel drive pickup truck, you could easily navigate the old roadbed about five miles - all the way to State Highway 3.

Time and time again Kade had found the gate damaged or completely pulled out of the ground, but had never been able to catch anyone in the act. Despite his efforts to make the gate "vandal proof," Kade had replaced or repaired it several times in the past few years and he was getting tired of that; not to mention the cost involved. This was a drain on his budget, having to spend money on the same thing – gate repairs or new gates, over and over again.

Maybe he and Phil should stop, talk with the six guys, and try to find out what they were doing. But Kade didn't like the looks of this situation, nor the odds. Plus, he was pretty sure these guys had guns and were drinking beer – not a good combination.

What a beautiful fall day, thought Kade Holley, as he readied his equipment and vehicle for a drive around the Marietta District. Mid-October in southeastern Ohio, sunny, trees in full color, temperatures in the low 70's – it didn't get any better than that. He was glad this was the day his boss had chosen to come over and see how things were going.

Phil Jones was the Forest Supervisor for the Wayne National Forest and he was one of the best bosses Kade had ever had - stern, but fair. He expected hard work and dedication to public service. Kade appreciated that. Phil had on-the-ground experience, too. He wasn't one of those ivory tower supervisors sent in here from the Regional Office or Washington, DC, who had little or no field experience. Phil had worked at National Forests in Wisconsin, Missouri, Virginia, and New Hampshire and had experience in fire, recreation, timber management, minerals, and public information.

Phil had grown up in Paducah, Kentucky and had attended forestry school at Purdue University in Indiana. Kade was a native West Virginian, attended that state's university in Morgantown, and had previous National Forest assignments in Minnesota, Georgia, and West Virginia. The two men hit it off from the first day they met.

Phil's office was about 90 miles away and he tried to come over and spend a day with Kade every few months. Of course, Phil supervised three Rangers, several program specialists in the main office, and was plenty busy trying to keep the Regional Headquarters in Milwaukee informed as to what was happening in Ohio. There were times he had to cancel planned visits, so when he did come over, they always tried to spend a full day to their advantage by looking at various projects in the area.

It was almost 9:00 a.m. when Kade saw Phil's vehicle turn off the main road out front and into the Ranger Station compound. Kade stepped inside to grab his radio and jacket, put his name on the sign-out board, and give his employees a heads up that Phil was here. Kade knew that Phil would come inside for a few minutes to say hello to everyone before they headed out for the day.

After a quick cup of coffee, some light conversation, and an update on what was new at the main office, Phil and Kade were ready to go. No sack lunches were needed this time. They would pass several places to eat on the route that Kade would be taking today. He had about five or six stops planned with specific items he wanted to discuss with Phil. They would also be passing the Winfield Run General Store around lunch time.

Whenever Phil came over, if at all possible, he liked to stop there and have them make him a "Winfield Run Special," a meal unto itself. Kade and Gale Payne, who owned the store, had more or less invented the sandwich on a whim one day and eventually Gale turned it into his trademark lunchtime offering. He sold between 10 and 20 of them every day.

The "special" was a triple decker sandwich on wheat, white, or rye, your choice. The top deck was a big stack of thin shaved ham, a slice of hot pepper cheese, and mustard; and the bottom deck was another big stack of thin turkey breast slices, Swiss cheese, and mayonnaise. Onions and pickles were optional, but Gale would put anything else you wanted on it; and he somehow put it all between three slices of bread. A "special" and something to drink were about all you needed for lunch.

Kade pulled his pickup truck out of the Ranger Station, onto the main road, and began explaining the day's plan to Phil. First, they would swing by the Maple Leaf Run Picnic Area and Boat Launch. Kade was pushing hard for funding to improve the area and turn it into an overnight campground. Development and construction dollars were definitely scarce, but Kade was convinced this project would be a big hit with the local public, as well as with those traveling through the area.

It was located on the banks of the Ohio River and that alone would be a big draw. There was no other developed campground along the river in this area on public land. Maple Leaf Run was really underutilized as a picnic area, despite the fact that there were two large pavilions located there, which were popular with groups for things like family reunions and school outings. The boat launch received fairly heavy use on the weekends, and some local people liked to hike, bird watch, and take photos in the area. But many of the individual picnic tables were seldom used.

Kade had done a lot of talking with various local groups about a possible campground at Maple Leaf Run. The school district officials, the Chamber of Commerce, the

Tourist and Convention Bureau, County Commissioners and Township Trustees, two bankers, three or four service organizations – everyone seemed to think it was an excellent idea. From the sketches Kade had done on his own, he knew they could improve the boat launch area, keep the two picnic shelters, turn the individual picnic locations into overnight campsites, add several additional sites, and even expand the hiking and bird watching areas.

The biggest audiences Kade had to convince in order for this project to move forward were his boss and those who worked at the Regional Office, which was located in Wisconsin and provided oversight to 15 or 16 national forests in 13 states. To Kade, it seemed like the larger national forests in New England, the upper Lake States, and Missouri almost always received preferential treatment for scarce funds over this small national forest in Ohio. But Kade was working hard to convince Phil that this campground was a good idea. Today would be another step in the right direction for the project. Kade had a good feeling about it.

Kade also wanted to show Phil a proposed site for an oil and gas well, which a local driller wanted to develop. The driller actually owned the mineral rights beneath the national forest at that location, but Kade and his staff had to approve the proposed well site location after considering all potential environmental impacts.

Then, Kade and Phil would head on over to the Little Muskingum River and stop to look at a couple of the small canoe access sites that were so popular with fishermen, hunters, and canoeists. There were four of these canoe access areas along a 35-mile stretch of the river and each one had three or four primitive campsites with a fire grill, garbage cans, and a pit toilet. Nothing fancy, but they were easy to maintain and received heavy use.

Kade and Phil spent the morning as planned. They had a good discussion about the potential campground project, checked the other areas, and had time to discuss various personnel, budget, and administrative issues. It was nearly Noon by the time they made it to the Winfield Run General Store.

As usual, Gale gave them a hearty welcome and asked, "What'll it be, rangers, a couple of Winfield Run Specials?"

"Better make it three," Phil said. "Kade and I want one now, and I'd like to take one home, too. This is the highlight of my day. And be sure to put pickles on mine." Gale liked Phil and he always smiled when Phil told him how much he looked forward to the Winfield Run Specials.

Gale Payne was an interesting person. Kade had known him now for five years and they had become good friends. Gale and his wife ran this store and the attached canoe livery, which was quite busy in the spring and summer. It was 25 miles to the nearest large grocery store, so Gale stocked quite a selection of groceries for area residents. He sold sandwiches and also carried a lot of basic hardware and farming items, as well as gloves, caps, work shirts, and other assorted clothing.

Gale had taught junior high school science for 15 years at a school a couple of hours north of here near Canton. He and his wife then moved back home to be near his mother when his dad had passed away about 12 years previous. Gale had planned to find a teaching position locally, but, instead, several long-time customers convinced him to continue operating the family store. To make ends meet, he dabbled in farming a little, and lately he had begun catering more to tourists, canoeists, hunters, and fishermen by stocking items they were likely to buy. They even held a special breakfast for hunters each morning of deer season.

The fishing was good in the Little Muskingum River; the smallmouth, largemouth, and spotted bass were plentiful. You could also catch bluegills, catfish, and crappie. The biggest prize of all, however, was the muskie. This river was one of just a handful in the state where you could catch native muskies. Gale's uncle had told Kade that he once saw a muskie in the river that was longer than a flat bottomed boat. Kade doubted that, but he had personally seen a few caught that pushed 40 inches in length.

Gale and his neighbors had not always viewed the national forest personnel as their friends. Many of the locals did not like the restrictions placed upon the use of national forest lands, and they were not happy when the forestry officials would purchase another piece of land from a private landowner to add to the forest. The purchases were always made on a "willing seller – willing buyer" basis, but still, some of the local residents did not like the changes that were occurring. Most of the changes were just normal social changes, but the "government" seemed to take a lot of the blame. "Dad-gum *gummint*," Kade had heard them say on more than one occasion, in their finest southeastern Ohio dialect.

Gale had fallen in with that group for several years, but since he and Kade had become friends, Kade had been able to clear up some of the misunderstandings and rumors that seemed to fly around. Gale had actually turned into a supporter of the national forest, as he began to see its many positive benefits. Many other neighbors, but not all, were coming around to Gale's way of thinking, too.

Kade worked well with the local residents. He understood them and tried to incorporate many of their ideas into his management activities. They appreciated that. At times when they had a complaint about the national forest, Kade had to admit that they were right. Kade didn't want to be one of those national forest rangers who came in from somewhere far away and ignored the suggestions of the local residents. After all, Kade thought, they live here. If we can't get along with our neighbors, maybe we shouldn't have a national forest here at all.

Kade and Phil finished their lunches and, as usual, Phil ended up buying a couple of difficult to find hardware items. "Can't hardly find these anymore," Phil never failed to remark, in his colorful western Kentucky style.

They said their goodbyes to Gale, and Kade thought he would swing by the canoe access site just on the other side of the Heldman Covered Bridge to make sure everything looked okay. There were five covered bridges still standing in the area and you could drive over three of them. You could park and look at the other two, and walk across them, if you wanted. The bridges ranged from 60 years to over 100 years old.

These were definite tourist attractions, with visitors coming to see them at all times of the year, often from quite a distance. Kade recalled an instance last summer when a retired couple from Texas had stopped by the office asking for directions. They had read about the area's covered bridges in a travel magazine. Another time, two middle-aged sisters from Vermont were vacationing in the Midwest and decided to drive across the bridges to compare them to those back home. They had learned about the covered bridges when they stopped by the welcome center in town.

Kade and Phil crossed the bridge and checked out the recreation area. Everything seemed to be fine this time, although vandalism had occurred at the site off and on for the past few years. Sometimes there was graffiti; once, a picnic table had been partially burned; and just last year the entrance sign had been stolen. Nothing appeared out of the ordinary this time, however, and for that, Kade was thankful.

Kade would now head toward the Ray's Run Natural Area and then he planned to stop by the Duker Ridge Timber Sale to see how it was progressing. That should put them back at the office in plenty of time for Phil to drive home before too late.

It would take about 20 minutes to get to Ray's Run, so Kade had plenty of time to remind Phil of the recurring problems they were having with the gate there.

Ray's Run was a Research Natural Area. It had been so

designated because of its unique characteristics, which included native white pine and a scattering of pitch pine. There were just a few remnant stands of native white pine in the area. Some foresters were skeptical that these stands were indeed native and thought the trees had been planted years ago. This, despite the early botanical records of the area that indicated white pine was present when some of the first scouts had traveled down the Ohio River to begin exploring what was known at the time as the "western frontier." Kade himself had studied the Ray's Run area closely and was convinced that it was definitely native white pine.

The pitch pine was not very common either. Mixed among the white pine, it formed a unique ecosystem with associated flowers, shrubs, and other plants. While not considered rare, this mix did not occur together very often. Several botanists, foresters, and other scientists from the Forest Service Research Station near Columbus, as well as Ohio State University and the Ohio Division of Natural Areas and Preserves, had received permits to conduct scientific studies of the area. This made it important to at least keep motorized vehicles out, in order to better protect the scientific studies.

It had only been about 30 years previous that foresters had begun to notice the unique botanical aspects of the area. Then it was just a few years before Kade arrived at this duty location from a previous assignment in Georgia, that a gate had been installed at the entrance. It wasn't meant to keep people out, especially hunters, because this had been a popular deer, grouse, and turkey hunting area for many years. But they now had to walk in; no vehicles were allowed. This lessened the chance for off-road disruption of the research study area. There were several informational signs in the area explaining the situation, as well as a brochure which was available at the District office.

People who drove down from the cities in the northern part of the state didn't seem to mind the gate. It was the locals who had driven that old dirt road for decades, all the way through to the state highway five miles away, who hated that gate. Kade had heard about it more than once from people who stopped by the office to complain. When he explained why the gate was there, most people understood; but there were a few who did not agree, and would never agree, with that gate being installed.

Kade felt good about the current gate. It was heavy duty with thick iron posts embedded in concrete deep in the ground. It had a heavy crossbar and locks on both sides that were hidden in cutouts barely big enough to get your hand in to unlock them. No way could you get a tool in there to cut these locks; plus they were case hardened, the best locks you could buy. Kade had seen evidence of a few attempts to knock over this gate, or pull it out of the ground......all to no avail.

He wanted to show this gate to Phil and talk a little bit about the whole situation. They might even have time to walk in a short ways to look at the unique pine ecosystem. Phil had never had a chance to view the area on the ground, although he had certainly read about it in the reports that Kade submitted monthly.

Kade turned off the state road and onto the gravel county road. It was just about a mile beyond this point to the Ray's Run Natural Area. As they drove around the final bend, Kade could see that there were three pickup trucks parked near the gate, one of them right in front of it. Oh no, he thought, not again. The closer he got, Kade could see several guys, six it looked like, carrying on, laughing, and appearing to be drinking.

As Kade slowed down to stop and see what was going on, two of the men quickly knelt down as if to hide. Just then, Kade caught a reflection off of what appeared to be a couple of rifles or shotguns. He couldn't be sure about the guns, but instinctively he gave the pickup a little gas and kept right on going. This situation did not look good – guns, beer drinking, and six-to-two odds. Kade doubted they were there to admire the positive merits of his newest gate design.

Kade explained to Phil what he was doing, and they both agreed that this was not a time to stumble into a bad situation. Kade made a quick radio call to the District office and to Marty Ervin, the District's Law Enforcement Officer. It turned out that Marty was with a county sheriff's deputy and the local Game Warden, who he had met for lunch. That afternoon, they had planned to investigate a possible litter/dumping violation not too far away and he radioed Kade that they could get to Ray's Run in about 10 minutes. Each of the officers was armed, well trained, and quite used to dealing with these types of situations.

They decided to take three separate vehicles, the deputy driving down from the northeast along the county road, and Marty and the Game Warden each coming up from the southwest direction. They would stop any pickup trucks they passed which were coming from the Ray's Run area. Marty and the Game Warden would pass the location where Kade and Phil were parked and have time to discuss the situation with them for a minute or two.

The deputy was the first to arrive at Ray's Run. When he got there, four of the men quickly jumped into two pickups to drive away, but the deputy pulled in at an angle to block their exit from the short entrance road. One of the pickups turned and drove up over the bank, straddled the ditch, and was just about to pull out onto the county road when Marty arrived and blocked his exit. The other pickup had backed up and rammed into the deputy's car, attempting to knock it out of the way to escape. Just then, the Game Warden arrived and further blocked that route.

As Kade and Phil arrived, a shot rang out, and the right front tire on their vehicle went flat. The two men closest to the gate turned and ran down the old Ray's Run road. Kade immediately recognized them as the angry father and son who had been in his office a month earlier complaining about the gate.

Upon hearing the gun shot, all three law enforcement officers drew their weapons, knelt behind their vehicles, and ordered the four men in the pickups to get out, hands held high. Thankfully, all four complied, although Kade thought, what choice did they have?

The officers frisked and cuffed all four of the men, placing three of them separately in the screened back seats of their cars. The fourth man was cuffed to the door of Kade's vehicle and the deputy made a radio call for backup help. Two additional sheriff's deputies were dispatched to the site and a state Highway Patrol officer was called to monitor the bottom end of the Ray's Run road in case the two men on foot made it all the way to State Highway 3. The officer was alerted that the men might be armed and that he should also stop anyone from walking in at the bottom end of the road.

It took the rest of the day to take the four men to jail and get a wrecker to haul the deputy's vehicle back to town. Luckily, Kade's vehicle sustained damage only to the tire. They changed it, and proceeded to the sheriff's office to make statements and fill out some papers. Later there would be more paperwork to fill out, lots of it – for the sheriff and also for the Forest Service reports that were required.

The Highway Patrol officer was eventually replaced by two deputy sheriffs, who kept watch for the two men on foot until well after dark. The men never showed up. Little matter, Kade thought, because he knew who they were, where they lived, and was sure they could be located within a few days at the most.

This nice, pleasant day, driving around the national forest, had quickly turned into a very dangerous situation and one that Kade would never forget. Of course, in his career as a forest ranger he had experienced many memorable situations; and he would experience more in the future. That was the life of a ranger. Never dull, sometimes dangerous, often memorable, and always fun. He loved it, all of it.

Oh, yes, the six men? The first four were brought up on

a variety of charges related to the incident at the Ray's Run Natural Area, including alcohol charges and, as it turned out, drug possession. The two who had rammed the deputy's car were on probation from earlier charges and each ended up serving six months in jail. The other two, due to some fancy "lawyering," as Phil described it, received 30-day suspended sentences and two years probation.

As Kade had predicted, the two men who ran away were soon captured. The father, Wade Tanner, was arrested at his home three days later without a struggle. The son, Jimmy Tanner, was pulled over for speeding in the next county, identified, and also arrested. They were both charged with five counts, including shooting at the forest rangers.

Marty Ervin had recovered a rifle and a shotgun from the site of the incident. He also took photos and collected as much evidence as he could from the area. Though both men denied having been at Ray's Run on that day, Kade's testimony at the trial, identifying the Tanners, was very convincing. Plus, the two men's fingerprints were all over the two guns. Marty also testified that the rifle had recently been fired. Then to top it off, when the three pickups had been thoroughly inspected by the deputies, they found six sticks of dynamite locked in the Tanners' toolbox. The dynamite, no doubt, had been intended for the gate.

Both men had several previous convictions, including disorderly conduct, speeding, driving under the influence, poaching, and assault. Due to the poaching conviction last summer, they were not supposed to be in possession of firearms for five years. The dynamite possession was illegal, of course, and despite their pleas that they had no idea how it had gotten in their toolbox, this really upset the judge. They were both convicted on four of the five charges brought against them and each sentenced to eight years in prison.

For the rest of the time Kade served as Ranger at this duty station, there was no attempt to vandalize the gate at Ray's Run Natural Area. And for the rest of their careers, even after retirement, whenever Kade and Phil would run into each other at meetings, conferences, or training sessions, they would talk about the years they had worked together in Ohio; how much they enjoyed being forest rangers; and yes, the day they almost got shot, in what they always referred to as - "the incident at Ray's Run."

Kade Holley, Forest Ranger

Chapter 3

Burn, Baby, Burn

Well, this was one fine fix Kade had gotten himself into. A simple prescribed burn had turned into a firetrap for the Ranger himself. Stupid, stupid, stupid was all he could think. There wasn't a lot of time to evaluate options. From what he knew of his location, the fuel conditions in front of him and on both sides, and the speed the fire was moving ..... there was only one thing he could do. And he probably had less than a minute to get it done.

It was a great day to live and work in the Piedmont of North Carolina, thought Kade Holley. Even though it was technically still winter, you could feel that springtime was right around the corner. The birds were chirpy today, and the trees seemed just about ready to burst into a new year of growth.

As always, it was also a great day to be a Forest Ranger. The workloads were heavy and danger was a constant companion, but Kade couldn't be happier with his chosen profession. This "piney woods" area of the South was certainly unlike his native West Virginia, but it was beautiful in its own right. The U.S. Forest Service had assigned Kade to various states during his career and each location was unique and interesting. Kade thought that each job he had done, and each state in which he had worked, combined to make him a better employee and a better Forest Ranger. Still, he often thought of West Virginia and always assumed that he would one day end up back in the Mountain State.

Today the weather service was calling for clear skies, light wind from the southwest, temperatures around 60 degrees, and average humidity for this time of year. Yes, it was going to be a perfect day to finally do that prescribed burn on the 200-acre tract of Uwharrie National Forest land located adjacent to the Fairhope Church Road.

Based upon weather predictions, future work projects, and availability of enough personnel to complete a burn of this size, Kade and his two primary fire specialists,

Donnie Ryder and Larry Kelley, had been tentatively planning to complete the fuel reduction burn near Fairhope Church today. Almost all of the District personnel, even the office staff, would be involved in one way or another; and two volunteer fire department (VFD) trucks, the sheriff's office, and the local EMT squad would assist as necessary. Everyone enjoyed these "burn" days, and even though it was hard work and usually called for long hours, they were all eager to get started.

A fuel reduction burn in this 35 year old stand of loblolly pine would accomplish several things. First, as the name implied, a prescribed burn would be conducted under carefully controlled and monitored conditions. It would reduce the amount of fuel that was on the ground. An accumulation of pine needles, twigs, and various other types of understory brush and vines could eventually lead to a major, damaging wildfire. Controlled and planned periodic burns in these stands greatly reduced that risk.

In addition, these prescribed burns were beneficial for wildlife. The lush growth that sprouted from the soil following these burns was a favorite browsing location for white-tailed deer. The wild turkeys in the area also liked it, for nibbling on flowers and buds, as well as eating the many insects and bees that seemed to come in following the fires. Plus, the loblolly pine trees would take a growth spurt in the years following the burn, and that was good for timber values.

The local church congregation and the few homeowners who lived just out the road approved of these burns, too. Most of them thought that the fires killed snakes, chiggers, and ticks; and this was a good thing in their minds. Kade always told folks that these types of fires did little to control those pests and scientific studies proved it. However, most of the local residents had been swayed for so long by their parents and grandparents that they were convinced the fires would control the snakes and bugs. There was no sense arguing with them about it, Kade concluded. Let them think what they want to on this topic. The controlled burns were good for many other reasons.

The one thing the neighbors would not be happy about, though, was heavy smoke in and around their homes. Thankfully, the southwest wind predicted for today would be perfect for carrying the smoke away from the church and the nearby homes.

Larry Kelley had prepared the burn plan for this project several weeks ago for Kade to approve. As part of the plan, Larry had calculated a range of temperatures, wind speeds, and relative humidity that would be necessary for this to be a safe and effective burn. Above or below the ranges for any of the three parameters, and

Kade would not give the final go ahead to light the fire. Wind direction was also critical, especially in this instance, plus it had to be dry enough since the last rain to enable the fire to burn fairly hot and accomplish their natural resource objectives.

Because any fire, planned or unplanned, was dangerous, the prescribed burn plan included safety requirements, backup assistance if needed, and it called for notification of several local and state agencies. The plan specified the number of employees required to conduct the burn and outlined their duties; how to control the fire or put it out, if that became necessary; and it listed radio frequencies so that all employees working on the fire could maintain contact with one another.

The Burn Boss for this prescribed burn would be Donnie, who was Kade's most experienced fire employee. Donnie Ryder had probably been involved with well over 100 controlled burns in his 25 year career, and at least that many wildfires, too. He knew the District like the back of his hand and he understood fire behavior extremely well. He insisted on safety considerations in everything he did. Larry was younger than Donnie and had worked under him for about 12 years now. He was somewhat better at the theoretical aspects of fire planning, and he was definitely more suited than Donnie to prepare the required paperwork.

With Donnie's field experience and level head, combined with Larry's theoretical and planning talents, Kade was sure he had the best fire team on the forest.

According to Larry's calculations in the burn plan, a fire of this size would require 16 District employees to carry it out safely and effectively. Donnie almost always thought this was overkill, because when he first started working on the forest, they would complete a burn of this size with seven or eight firefighters, even five or six on occasion. Technically, he was probably right, but with all the recent emphasis on safety and various natural resource requirements, Kade always leaned toward having more people involved rather than too few. There were so many things that could go wrong when you were dealing with fire that sufficient help was always reassuring to Kade. Most of Larry's burn plans also called for two VFD crews and trucks to be strategically located for backup support in case the fire started behaving differently than planned. They were paid a modest fee for their standby presence; and if they ended up being called in to help put out an escaped fire, they were paid the standard rates for fighting a wildfire.

Kade had known a District Ranger in the Lake States and one in the Deep South who had each let a prescribed burn escape their control and turn into a large wildfire. The one in the south ended up burning 275 additional acres, mostly on private land, before they got it under control. It nearly cost the Ranger his job, but he was able to weather the storm and keep his career intact with only a reprimand in his personnel file.

The other story in the Lake States was an entirely different matter. In that instance, they had elected to go ahead and start their prescribed burn under marginal conditions and didn't take into proper account the fact that the weather prediction for later that day was even worse. Kade was certain that Larry would not let something like that happen today, as he had responsibility for making the final recommendation to Kade on whether or not to "light" the Fairhope Church burn.

That Lake States fire ended up burning several thousand acres and took five days to get it under control. It burned up three homes, a dozen cabins, five or six vehicles, some barns and outbuildings, and it was a miracle that no one was killed. The Governor's Office and Forest Service Headquarters were not happy, to say the least. The Ranger was found responsible for the situation, demoted, and reassigned to an office job at another national forest. Kade had known him at a previous duty assignment and had always liked him. He never regained his former confidence; and his morale suffered after the reassignment. He seemed to simply be going through the motions of his current job, waiting until he could retire in a few years. Kade felt sorry for him, but understood that there were ramifications to mishandling these fire situations. That's why it was so critical to plan and carry out these prescribed burns as carefully and safely as possible. Kade never took any shortcuts or chances with them.

Last week, Larry and two of his crew had taken the District's dozer out to the burn area and "freshened up" the perimeter control lines. They cleared away all the limbs, leaves, pine cones, and trees that had fallen onto or across the lines. This morning, a quick trip around the perimeter on a four-wheeler would ensure that the lines were ready. If they did find anything lying on the fire line, they would remove it or send a crew to take care of it before the prescribed burn was lit.

Kade had all the District personnel come in at 7:00 a.m. the day of the burn to get things ready, such as equipment, fuel, personal protective gear, and vehicles, and to hold a mandatory safety briefing. Duties and responsibilities were covered and they went over the weather forecast. Escape routes and safety zones were also verified and discussed. By 8:30 a.m. everyone was on their way to the location; twenty minutes and they would be there. The light fog had lifted and the dew was quickly drying. Kade hoped that by 10:00 a.m., or shortly thereafter, there would be fire on the ground.

The gathering spot and the command center would be located in the church parking lot. Pastor Edwards was a close friend of Kade's. In fact, the two families had attended a professional basketball game in Charlotte a month earlier and were planning a baseball trip to Atlanta to watch the Braves play in May. Edwards was quite a sports fan and was also always willing to assist in any way he could with national forest activities.

Around 9:30 a.m., Larry took the on-site weather measurements and called the Weather Service for a spot forecast. Everything checked within acceptable parameters and Donnie was ready for a test burn. He took three men with him up into the edge of the burn area for the test fire and returned within 15 minutes, satisfied that the burn would proceed as expected. Radios were all checked, frequencies confirmed, and final instructions were given before all firefighters headed to their assigned positions. It was a couple of minutes before 10:00 a.m. when Larry advised Kade that everything was in place for a successful burn. Kade gave Donnie the "go-ahead" to begin.

The 200-acre parcel was rectangular in shape and relatively flat. There was one small creek that bisected the tract, forming a ravine that was probably 15 feet deep in a few spots. The fire would not burn down into those deeper areas, nor was it necessary that it did so in order to accomplish the objectives of the prescribed burn. There was probably a foot of water in the creek in several of those sections and from bank to bank it averaged about 30 feet across.

Drip torches would be used to light fire strips across the tract, approximately 20 feet apart, beginning at the northeast end and working back into the slight wind, which was coming from the southwest. That would help keep the fire burning under a slow rate of spread. The firing crew would "strip" a line right across the creek in most places, except where the ravine was too deep. They would simply go around those areas until the ravine became shallow and pick back up with lighting their strips.

Sometimes during prescribed burns, when it was safe to do so, Kade would walk out into the area which had already burned to check on the intensity of the fire to ensure that it was burning hot enough to accomplish the objectives of the prescription. If the fire burned too hot, there could be damage to the residual trees; or in extreme cases some of them could even be killed. If the fire burned too cool, not enough of the accumulated fuel would be burned off, defeating the primary purpose of the prescribed burn. This one seemed to be going just about right and Kade figured he would walk out into the burned area and check on things by around Noon.

Listening to the radio chatter, Kade could tell that

things were proceeding as planned and that by about 2:00 p.m. they hoped to wrap up the active burn. Of course, after that the crews would walk back through to make sure there were not any significant unburned areas. If they found any, they would usually burn those out. There would also be some spot mop-up of stumps and heavy smoldering logs to ensure these wouldn't eventually flare back up and send sparks or embers across the control line into unburned forest. A couple of four-wheelers would drive the entire perimeter to ensure that things looked okay and that a "spot" fire hadn't escaped across the line somewhere unintended. Usually there were one or two of these, and today was no exception. One small "spot" or crossover would be detected later that afternoon and quickly put out before it reached even a tenth of an acre in size. These situations were almost always easily contained when there were enough personnel on hand and when prescribed fires were conducted within appropriate weather conditions.

Just before noon, Kade decided to walk out and inspect the burn results. It was fairly smoky, but no worse than he had experienced on numerous other occasions. He tied a wet bandana across his nose and mouth for easier breathing. From what he could see to this point, the burn results were satisfactory.

Before long, Kade had proceeded to where he could see

the fire and several of the crew members at work, although he was fairly certain they had not seen him. No need to bother them or distract them, he thought. Kade noticed a point where the fire strip was uneven because the crew had gone around a steep ravine. He jumped across the creek at a narrow point into an unburned area and walked down the other side, figuring to cross back over once the ravine became shallower in a couple of hundred feet.

Kade lost visual contact with the crew, but he didn't think much about it. He would call on his radio in a few minutes to let them know his location. Before he had a chance to do so, however, and before he fully realized what was happening, Kade felt a rush of heat from his left. He turned and saw a rapidly moving 10-15 foot wall of flame bearing down on him. Unknowingly, he had walked beyond the firing crew, which was unaware that Kade was there. They were "tying-in" the burn strip to the ravine, where they had stopped on the other side. Yes, Kade was in a fix. The fire was burning too hot to go back through it into a "safe" area that was already burned; and it was moving too fast to outrun it to safety.

I am stupid, Kade thought, as he felt an adrenaline surge. I've gotten myself into a firetrap. Quickly evaluating options, and thinking back to the safety briefing, Kade decided the only thing he could do was jump down into the ravine and let the fire pass, hopefully without burning him in the process. Luckily, this was one of the steeper portions of the ravine and there was standing water in the creek. He half jumped, half slid down the hill and splashed some water on his bandana and his face. It couldn't have been more than 30 seconds before the wall of flame came roaring past his location on the flat area above him. Kade felt a surge of heat and the creek bank vibrated. He heard a dull roar as the fire passed beyond him. The sheer power and energy of a fire always amazed Kade.

Kade was going to be all right, he knew. He would only have been in danger of injury or death if he had stayed up on the flat. One of the escape areas, which he had stressed to the crew during the pre-fire safety briefing, was to go down into the ravine, if there was no other option. Kade had done the right thing, and it all worked as planned. But one thing for sure, his pulse rate had jumped for several minutes, and the way his clothes were soaked, he must have lost about a gallon of sweat. He sat down on the bank of the creek, drank about half of the water from the canteen on his belt, and he gathered his thoughts.

Smoke had begun to accumulate in the ravine, so Kade took one last drink of water and then placed the bandana over his face, before climbing back up out of the ravine and walking into the burned over area. The flames were far in front of him now, and there was no danger. Kade inspected a little more of the burn results, careful to not get too close to the fire ahead.

After several minutes, content that the fire was accomplishing everything that was planned, Kade walked out to one of the control lines and then back to the parking lot. There he joined Larry, who was talking with one of the standby VFD crews at their fire truck. Larry was monitoring the fire progress by radio and supervising two of the District's senior citizen employees, who had been ferrying vehicles back and forth to pre-determined locations for the fire crews to drive after the burn was completed. Donnie was still out with the fire crews, directing, supervising, and monitoring what they were doing.

Kade told Larry that from his inspection, the burn was looking good. Maybe it was just his imagination, but Kade sensed that Larry suspected something had just happened. For one thing, Kade had never called in on his radio, and that was unlike him. But Kade never let on, figuring that no good would come of it. It would be at least another hour before the main part of the burn was over; then would come the "mop-up" duties and fire line inspections, before the crews would head back to the office. It would take another hour or more from that point to clean tools and put away as much equipment as they could. Other final items would be completed tomorrow morning. All in all it would be a long, but successful day.

Neither Larry, Donnie, nor any of the crew ever mentioned anything to Kade about what had happened; Kade didn't bring it up either. He guessed that they didn't know, but was never certain. It was not like Kade to get into such a situation as he did on this fire; and it was not like him to keep things from his key personnel. But he weighed the pros and cons and decided it was the best way to handle the situation this time. Since he had followed the safety plan for escape areas that was outlined in the pre-fire briefing, he felt like things had gone pretty much as planned. Certainly that was true for the rest of the prescribed burn.

However, this occurrence did make an impression on Kade to the point that he was more careful than ever around fires. He would emphasize, even more so than before, the importance of escape routes and safety areas in all fire activities for the rest of his career.

As always, Kade was thankful that he was a Forest Ranger. It was an important, exciting, and fulfilling career. Yes, it was sometimes dangerous, but he wouldn't have it any other way.

Kade Holley, Forest Ranger

Chapter 4

Lucky Ol' Me

What had to be the biggest, fattest copperhead he had ever seen was basking in the sun, not more than 10 feet from Kade's truck. He knew he shouldn't kill it and he certainly wouldn't, but it made him uneasy knowing that by the time he walked in to complete his job for the day and came back out, that snake would still be there – somewhere close by.

"If it weren't for bad luck, I'd have no luck at all." How many times had Kade Holley heard his Dad say that? Fifty or sixty? A hundred? Definitely too many to count; and here he was, in another jam on Thursday. It was the fourth time this week. Southern Ohio and the Wayne National Forest were great places to work, Kade thought, but this was getting to be a little bit ridiculous.

If he got out of this situation intact, Kade promised himself he was definitely going to take the day off on Friday. It didn't even matter that it was going to be Friday the 13th. Of course, since it **was** going to be Friday the 13th, there was no sense in tempting fate; but even if it was going to be the 1st, 30th, or any other day of the month, it wouldn't matter, he would still take it off.

Yep, his luck this week had all been bad, but he was still unhurt and alive, at least so far. It wasn't like Kade Holley had led a sheltered life or that he had never been in tense situations before. No, that wasn't close to being the case. He was, after all, a Forest Ranger and by the very nature of his job he was often exposed to danger. Heck, from time to time he even encountered situations that could possibly get him killed if they weren't handled properly. But this week, it was getting just a little ridiculous. Four days in a row? No way!

The snake thing on Monday had been totally his fault. No doubt about that. But still, in a hundred years how many times would a copperhead crawl up on a vehicle and slide into the cab of a pickup truck through an open window? It was probably a first, Kade thought. He never even dreamed a snake could do that. Yet, in retrospect he remembered having seen snakes crawl and slither up trees, houses, boats, and rock cliffs. No doubt they could climb a truck, too, if they wanted to.

Yes, based upon what he now knew, he should definitely have rolled up those windows. But at the time, he figured it was warm, sunny, with no clouds and he was more than a mile off the main road, parked behind a Forest Service gate. No sense rolling the windows up, he had thought. What a bad decision that was!

Kade needed to collect forestry data up in the Left Fork of Barnett Run. He had parked his pickup truck at the end of an old woods road near the bottom of the hill. The Forest Service required that various types of tree and forest information be updated every ten years. The National Forest lands in and around Barnett Run were scheduled for re-inventory this year.

It would take several weeks for Kade to take the measurements, collect all the data, enter it into the computer, update the maps, and so forth. There were numerous side drainages and hollows feeding into the main Barnett Run, and altogether there were over 5,000 acres of national forest land that he would need to update this year. He tried to schedule activities so that he could complete the field work on days like today, when the weather was good.

After Kade had parked his truck, put on his hardhat and vest, gathered the various forestry tools he would need for that day, and grabbed his lunch, he walked over to the edge of the creek. Almost instantly, he spotted the snake, one of the biggest, fattest copperheads he had ever seen. It was laying along the far edge of the creek on a big, flat rock where the rays of the morning sun shined directly on it.

Kade had never liked snakes, although he was not really concerned about walking in areas where they would likely be around. Heck, over the years he had encountered numerous copperheads and rattlesnakes, a few water moccasins, and plenty of non-poisonous snakes, too.

Kade had never been bitten, although he had stepped on a copperhead one time, and that mad dude had left fang marks on his boot. Kade even came face to face with a rattlesnake a few years previous, as he crawled on his belly to get closer to a stream without scaring the brook trout he was trying to catch. Of course, he also had a rattlesnake uncoil and lunge toward him once. Though it certainly startled him, it had missed his leg by a foot or more. He just considered those types of things as part of the job of being a Forest Ranger.

After spotting the big, fat copperhead, and making the decision to leave it alone and get out of there, Kade proceeded up the Left Fork of Barnett Hollow to complete his work for the day. He never even gave a second thought to having left the truck windows open.

Kade collected information on tree species, age, heights, diameters, stand density, and overall condition. He made notes on soil types, aspect, slopes, rock outcrops, springs, and always looked for signs of insect or disease problems. He wrote down comments about wildlife, including food and water sources, overall habitat conditions, and took note of such things as den trees, roost trees, and perch trees. By the time Kade was done and he had recorded all of his information back in the office, anyone who examined the data would have a very good idea of what the forest was like in that area.

Around Noon, Kade opened his sack lunch and ate. He was hungry and the two sandwiches didn't last long – one was bologna and cheese, and the other was peanut butter and jelly (actually it was strawberry jam). He ate the small container of tapioca pudding and drank about half of the bottled water; he would save the apple for a snack later in the afternoon. It wouldn't take much more than another hour to complete his field work for the day, and with a little luck he would have time to organize the day's findings back in the office. That would make it easier to complete the paperwork part of the job next week, when storms were predicted for the area and office work was required.

Less than two hours later, Kade was back at his pickup truck and ready to head back to the ranger station. He walked over to the edge of the creek and noticed that the copperhead was no longer around. Probably off hunting for lunch, Kade thought. He walked over to the pickup to unload his hardhat and gear on the passenger side and that was a lucky thing. Tossing his vest and gear on the passenger seat, and reaching in to lay his hardhat on the floor, he nearly jumped out of his boots when he saw the head and eyes of a snake peering out at him from the floor on the driver's side. He banged his head on the door frame as he turned rapidly and jumped backward away from the truck. His heart was thumping in his chest.

Kade regained his composure, took a couple of deep breaths, and slowly looked around the truck door, ready for anything. The snake was still there; other than the gentle sway of its head and its darting tongue, it had not moved at all.

Kade grabbed a shovel out of the truck bed and went around the other side to open the driver's door, taking care to keep the door between himself and the snake. He could see that it was definitely the copperhead from earlier in the day, and it sure appeared to be getting agitated. It was now in a more coiled position, looking out past the driver's door, and the top several inches of the snake were now lifted up and swaying. It seemed to be ready to strike at anything that came within range.

He would kill it if he had to, Kade thought, but he didn't really want that to happen. He went back around to the passenger side and, after making sure the snake was not waiting there to bite him (you know how your mind gets when things like that happen), he gently prodded the snake out the driver's side door. The way the copperhead moved, it seemed as happy to be leaving that scene as Kade was happy to have it go. It slithered down the road about 20 feet or so and then veered off toward the creek and over the bank. The snake was probably four or five feet long and had a thick body, as large a copperhead as Kade had ever seen in the wild. He was more than relieved and happy to have this situation behind him. And he vowed to himself to never leave his truck windows open like that again.

On Tuesday, Kade had gotten stuck in a ditch out on the bypass. No huge problem there, except the embarrassment of having to call Eddie Gale on the radio to come and pull him out. But there was a little more to the story than that.

Eddie had a smile on his face when he got there and snickered two or three times during the process of pulling "the Ranger" out of the ditch. Finally, Kade could take it no longer and explained to Eddie how he had rounded the curve and faced two cars, seemingly racing each other, and heading straight toward him. The only thing Kade could do was to hit the brakes and drive off the side of the road into the ditch. Luckily, it wasn't a dangerous drop-off, but it was a wet, swampy type of ditch and he immediately became stuck. After several unsuccessful tries at backing out of the situation, Kade had given up and called Eddie on the radio.

The Wednesday situation was somewhat unusual. Kade had taken his camera to the Orchard Mountain overlook to snap a few shots. He did this several times a year during different seasons to add to the District's photo file. These came in handy to use for brochures, displays, and for helping decorate the walls of the conference room in the Ranger Station.

After taking his last photo, Kade had noticed a slight movement in the fork of a large tree just over the edge of the hill. As he walked toward the tree and got closer, Kade realized that it was a raccoon. He quickly readied his camera, hoping to snap a few shots before the raccoon saw him and scurried away. He took about 10 photos, each one a step or two closer to the animal than the previous photo. By then, he was within 10 feet of the seemingly oblivious raccoon. All of a sudden it whirled around and snarled at Kade, catching him off guard and actually giving him quite a scare.

Kade knew enough to back away quickly from this situation because wild animals can be very unpredictable; and as he did so, the raccoon continued to snarl and shake its head. It was then that Kade noticed the white foam dripping from its mouth and he realized what was going on – the coon was rabid.

He was about halfway back to his truck when the coon jumped down from the tree and ran directly at Kade. This put quite a scare into Kade and he turned to run to the truck. Glancing back at the raccoon, he saw it running at him, but still quite a distance away. All of a sudden the raccoon fell and tumbled, rolling over several times. No sooner had it gotten back up than it fell down again. This was definitely a case of rabies, Kade thought. Rabies was not uncommon in this area of southeastern Ohio, but it was not often that anyone had an encounter such as this.

After Kade started the truck and turned it around to drive away, he looked across the open area and saw the raccoon lumbering unsteadily back toward the forked tree. From what Kade knew, the animal would be dead within a day or two at most. Though he was never close to being bitten or scratched, the situation had been a little unnerving to say the least. Kade would certainly alert all of his District personnel about what had happened and also use this incident as a lesson during the next monthly safety meeting.

Kade also called the state Game Protector and the

District Wildlife Office to report what had happened. They kept track of rabies reports around the state. The Game Protector went out the next day to the location Kade had told him about, but found no sign of the rabid raccoon. It had likely crawled away and died somewhere over the hill.

And now here he was on Thursday, when he figured that nothing else could go wrong, in probably a worse situation than he had been in all week. What he thought would be nothing more than a leisurely drive up Jacks Run to check on a new gas well that was being drilled, had turned into a precarious situation.

The Jacks Run Road was about a mile long, not particularly steep, and was generally in good condition. Kade had driven it probably a hundred times in the past and had never experienced a problem. The drill rig and other equipment for the well had been brought in on the Scooter Ridge Road, which was wider, flatter, and generally better suited for hauling large equipment. So, it wasn't like the Jacks Run Road had been damaged by heavy equipment or was in bad shape.

About halfway up the road, there was a slight curve to the right and a fairly steep drop off on the left. It was the only place along the road that Kade ever felt could cause a problem, but he generally just gave his truck a little gas and rolled easily past it to a short straight stretch, and then right on up to Scooter Ridge. But not this time, not this week. No, this was the week of bad luck and unbelievable craziness.

As Kade rounded the curve and gassed the truck slightly, he saw a large rock that had slid from the bank and was just where his right tire was heading. Instinctively, he swerved left to miss the rock, only to suddenly realize that he had gotten very close to the left edge of the road. He pulled the steering wheel sharply to the right, but it was too late; the back left tire had skidded over the edge of the road. He gassed it again figuring, incorrectly, that this would pull the entire truck back up onto the road. Maybe if he had been in 4-wheel drive that would have been the case. But it was too late to think about that now. Instead, it only served to further twist the vehicle and if he hadn't quickly slammed on the brakes, both rear tires would have ended up off the road. That had nearly happened and he was setting almost perpendicular to the road by this time.

But that wasn't the worst part, as he began to sense the wobbling, teetering movement of the truck. And just great, Kade thought; this was the steep drop off, too. He braced himself, preparing to roll down the slope with the truck. But nothing happened, except, of course, for the wobbling and teetering, which seemed to last forever. After what seemed like an hour, but was probably less than a minute, the truck quit rocking. Kade was almost afraid to move, thinking that this would cause the truck to go over the hill.

After awhile, Kade calmed down and began to consider his options. He could wait until someone came along; a few cars traveled that road each day and he figured that one would eventually show up. He could slide over and get out the passenger's side, but with the way the truck was balanced, he wasn't sure that was a good idea. Or he could call for help on the Forest Service radio. He hated to do that if there were other options, but it seemed the prudent thing to do in this case. So, reluctantly, Kade tried to radio the office. But as fate would have it, he was still deep enough in the hollow for the hill to block the reception to the radio tower. He tried to call several times with no success.

Finally, frustrated and a little unsure of what to do next, he honked the truck's horn. He held it down for 20 or 30 seconds. He let up and then repeated the effort – three more times. In a few minutes he saw two oil and gas workers walking down the road toward his truck. They surveyed the situation and talked with Kade to get his opinion before leaving to get their bulldozer.

Within 10 minutes they were back with the dozer, had connected their winch to the truck frame, and pulled the vehicle back up, fairly easily, onto the road again.

They also pushed the large rock, which had caused this whole situation, off the road and over the hill. Good riddance, Kade thought.

The whole situation had lasted less than an hour, but truth be told, to Kade it seemed like an all day ordeal. He was worn out. If the truck had slid or rolled over and down the hill, who knows what would have happened. It was probably close to 200 feet to the bottom from where the truck had been located, and the two most likely outcomes for Kade would have been death or serious injury. With that on your mind for an hour, who wouldn't be worn out?

After getting pulled back onto the road, he thanked the two men profusely and then followed the dozer back up to the top of the hill. The pickup seemed none the worse for wear and after checking it out the best he could, Kade made a slow, careful drive out Scooter Ridge to the county road and then back to the office.

Usually, Kade would just think, "another day, another adventure." But with four close calls in four days, he was true to his promise and looking forward to taking off the next day, Friday the 13th.

Being a Forest Ranger was a great job, no doubt about it. This week had put another wrinkle on Kade's face though, and a few more gray hairs on his head. But a day of rest and relaxation on Friday, a two-day weekend to get caught up with things around the house, and he'd be ready once again Monday to do the job he loved – being a Forest Ranger for the U.S. Forest Service.

Chapter 5

The Mount St. Helens Assignment

*Kade thought he would go ahead and take the fire
assignment. But first he wanted to touch base with his wife.
No sense heading west for 2-3 weeks without making sure the
family was fine with it. The Supervisor's Office had called
early Friday morning to see if he was interested in serving as
Crew Boss on a fire detail, probably to Montana or Idaho.
But now this. Just before lunch, as Kade was working on
some end-of-the-week reports and paperwork, another
opportunity arose. And he had until Monday morning to let
the Regional Office know whether or not he would be
available to lead a five-person team going to the Gifford
Pinchot National Forest in Washington – to assist that Forest*

with recreation and visitor information duties at Mount St. Helens. What an interesting opportunity!

Kade Holley had a lot of office work to catch up on, so he went in a little early on Friday. He wasn't crazy about the paperwork part of the job, but he knew it was important. He always did his best with reports and documentation of projects that had been completed. About an hour into his work, Kade got a call from the Supervisor's Office.

It was the Fire Staff Officer, Herbie Hughes, checking to see if Kade was available to serve as Crew Boss on a western fire assignment next week. The initial word was that this crew would be sent to either Montana or Idaho. Hughes wanted to line up a Crew Boss before he put together the rest of the crew.

This 20-person crew would be made up of a combination of state and federal employees from Ohio, and possibly five or six Forest Service employees from Indiana. They wouldn't have to fly out until the middle of next week, so Herbie told Kade he could have until Monday morning to let him know.

It was now mid-August and this would be the third crew the Wayne National Forest had sent to support western firefighting efforts this summer. Actually, the first two crews had been made up of employees from the Forest

Service, as well as employees from the Ohio Division of Forestry. The two agencies worked closely on many projects, but particularly on firefighting.

The first crew had flown into Spokane, Washington in July and was then sent by bus to the Kaniksu National Forest in northern Idaho. The Crew Boss was Hawk Thompson, one of Kade's friends and fellow rangers from an adjacent District. They spent five days working on that fire before being sent, again by bus, to the Interagency Fire Center in Boise to await a further assignment.

After a day to rest and re-group, the crew was sent to the Challis National Forest in east-central Idaho to help fight a large fire that was burning in a remote area. That was the "big one" that everyone had seen mentioned on numerous TV reports for several weeks. The fire was burning in steep and rugged country, requiring a considerable distance for the firefighting crews to hike in and out each day. It took several hundred firefighters to finally bring the blaze under control.

No sooner had that crew returned home than another crew was dispatched to southern California to help with a fire on the Angeles National Forest. Whereas the Idaho fires had burned in big timber country with Douglas-fir and Engelmann spruce, the southern California fire was burning mostly in chaparral, manzanita, and other "brush," with some scattered Coulter pine and sugar pine.

The fire had destroyed several homes and took over 2,000 firefighters to finally bring it under control. It was a dangerous, fast-moving fire and the heavy smoke was contributing to the serious air pollution problems that southern California had already been experiencing.

Kade had been tied up with important projects previously that summer, plus he had some family obligations, so they hadn't pressured him to go west earlier. But now, since he was the most experienced Crew Boss on the Forest, Kade was sure that the Forest Supervisor and the Fire Staff Officer would expect him to take this assignment. It was the duty of Forest Service employees from all across the country to pitch in and help out during emergencies, especially forest fires.

Kade had two reports to complete before lunch and he definitely wanted to finish one before he called his wife about the fire assignment. About mid-morning, as he was close to completing his first report, the District Clerk, Dorene Timmons, buzzed Kade's phone and told him there was a call from Neal Charlton in the Regional Office (RO).

Kade had known Neal for several years. He was currently in charge of the Public Information program in Milwaukee, and before that he had served in a variety of Recreation assignments across the country, both at the national forest level and in the RO. "Any idea what he wants?" Kade asked.

"No, he wouldn't tell me," replied Dorene. "I kept asking him, but he just said it was important and that he needed to talk with you now."

"Okay, transfer the call through," said Kade. "After that, if you would, hold my calls the rest of the morning. I have a report to complete and then I need to call my wife about that fire assignment they want me to go on next week. Herbie wants me to let him know my decision by early Monday morning, but I hope to get back to him with an answer later this afternoon."

"Okay," said Dorene. "When I hang up, Mr. Charlton will be on Line 2."

Kade answered Neal's call and the two old friends exchanged greetings and small talk for a couple of minutes. "I hate to cut it short, Neal. You know how much I enjoy talking with you," said Kade. "But I have a couple of important things to finish and then decide about a western fire assignment that the Supervisor's Office wants me to go on next week."

"Funny you should mention that," said Neal. "In a roundabout way that's exactly what I need to talk with you about."

"Now I'm confused," Kade said. "Why are you involved with western fire assignments?"

"Well," Neal explained, "we had a short staff meeting this morning here in Milwaukee to discuss a request we received from our counterparts out in the Portland Regional Office. As you know, our Regional Forester and theirs are long-time friends. Anyway," Neal continued, "they would like us to send a five-person team to help them out with some recreation and visitor center duties at Mount St. Helens on the Gifford Pinchot National Forest. To make a long story short, your name came up as a possible team leader for that assignment."

"Well, I'm honored, I guess," said Kade, "but it seems like there would be some recreation staff officers around the Region who would be more qualified than a District Ranger. Plus, why do they need folks from other Regions to help out with something like this?"

"Couple of reasons why your name came up," Neal replied. "First, we need a Team Leader, someone with experience supervising people, someone similar to a

Crew Boss on a fire detail. This team will be helping those folks with their recreation duties because they're short-handed right now, but the team will also be evaluating and making recommendations on a couple of the Gifford Pinchot forest's recreation activities. Naturally, we need a Team Leader who can coordinate this and put together good reports that will be meaningful and helpful to them," said Neal.

"One thing for sure," replied Kade sarcastically, "I do know how to write reports. It seems like that's all I get done anymore."

"The other thing," Neal continued, "is that we know you have had experience working at Visitor Centers in Minnesota and Georgia. At least a week of this assignment will be evaluating operations at their new Visitor Center near Mount St. Helens and helping them with the heavy workload they expect over the Labor Day holiday."

"And as far as why they need help from another Region," explained Neal, "they have sent so many people to help out with fires in other western states this year that they are extremely short-handed right now. In fact, they still have several employees currently working in other states, including most of their normal visitor center staff, who are working down in Wyoming in the Yellowstone area. This has been one of the worst fire seasons in the West in several years and everyone out there is stretched pretty thin."

"Now that you've explained things, it all makes sense," said Kade. "It would definitely be an interesting opportunity, but the Supervisor's Office wants me to lead a crew on a western fire detail. I have to let them know no later than Monday morning, but I'm pretty sure the Forest Supervisor expects me to do it. I was actually hoping to give them an answer later this afternoon after talking things over with my wife."

"That fits our timeline, too," Neal said. "If you decide to accept this recreation assignment, the Regional Forester will explain things to your Forest Supervisor and Fire Staff Officer. This would be a huge favor to the folks out in Washington. To be honest, I think our Regional Forester expects you to do this, but you know how he is. He wants willing participants and doesn't like to force people to do things against their will."

"Let me think it over and talk with my wife at lunchtime," Kade said. "I'd like to get this all settled today and not wait until Monday. That will give me time to wrap up some things around the house this weekend. I'll call you back right after lunch."

"That will be great," said Neal, "Talk with you later today."

With all of these things on his mind, Kade was still able to get his two reports finished before lunch time. And instead of calling his wife Lynn on the phone, he decided to go home for lunch. They had a lot to discuss.

As usual, Lynn was very supportive and left the final decision up to Kade. But she did tell him that since fire assignments were always dangerous, she would be much less worried if he were working in a Visitor Center in Washington; even though it was close to where a volcano had blown off the side of a mountain several years previous. Their three kids would all be in school, so it would be a little less work on her with Kade being gone than it would have been earlier in the summer.

On the way back to the office Kade had pretty much decided to take the recreation detail to the Gifford Pinchot National Forest. He was very interested in it and these types of opportunities didn't come along very often. He could go on a fire assignment just about every year if he wanted to. Still, he was a little concerned about how the Supervisor's Office would react.

Kade decided he would give Herbie Hughes a heads-up before he called Neal Charlton in the Regional Office.

So, Kade called the Supervisor's Office. "Hi Herbie,"

Kade said. "About that fire assignment...." Kade continued.

"Hold on," Herbie interrupted, "let me tell you that I'm already aware of the Regional Office request for you to go to Mount St. Helens. And we're 100 percent okay with it, if that's what you want to do. I guess the Regional Forester didn't want us to be blind-sided, so he called the Forester Supervisor just a short while ago. They agreed that you were more needed to go to the Gifford Pinchot National Forest than this fire assignment. We have a couple of other Crew Boss qualified people around here who can lead a fire crew."

"Well, that makes it a little easier for me," Kade said. "I just didn't want you guys in the Fire Shop to be upset with me."

"Not a problem," said Hughes. "We'll tap you for one of the first Crew Boss assignments next fire season."

"I appreciate it Herbie," replied Kade. "Let me hang up and call Neal Charlton in the Regional Office. He's coordinating this recreation assignment."

"Good luck with everything," said Herbie, "and don't get too close to that volcano out there."

"I certainly won't do that," Kade laughed. "I'll talk with you when I get back and let you know how things went."

Kade hung the phone up and immediately called Charlton in the Regional Office. "I guess I'll be headed to Mt. St. Helens, if you still want me," Kade told Neal.

"Still want you? I was actually counting on it," said Neal. "I heard that the Regional Forester called your boss to pave the way. I already have four probable team members lined up to go with you."

"You sure work fast, Neal. Who are they?" Kade asked.

"It looks like it will be a Recreation Specialist from the Green Mountain National Forest in Vermont; a Visitor Center Interpretive Specialist from West Virginia on the Monongahela National Forest; a District Clerk from the Ottawa National Forest in Michigan, who is involved heavily in visitor information services; and a Landscape Architect from the Allegheny National Forest in Pennsylvania. I've actually been putting together the team for the past few days, but we hadn't settled on a Team Leader yet. We wanted to make sure we got the right person for that," explained Neal, "and now it looks like we have him."

"I appreciate that, Neal. What's the timeline on the travel? Hopefully not tomorrow morning," Kade joked.

"No," laughed Neal, "but we would like for all five of you to fly into Portland, Oregon on Tuesday and meet with the Gifford Pinchot's Recreation Staff Officer that evening at your hotel just across the river in Vancouver, Washington. That's their Supervisor's Office Headquarters. The Staff Officer is Ron Perez. I worked with him years ago in California. He's a former District Ranger, a great guy, and has worked on the Gifford Pinchot National Forest for 10 or 12 years. He'll give you a run down on what they expect from you, where you'll be staying, and all of the arrangements on that end."

"That's about all I know," Neal continued. "Ron did say that since you'll be there for several days before Labor Day that he would probably begin with a recreation assignment and have you lodged at a small motel in the town of Cougar just on the south side of the National Volcanic Monument."

"After you complete your work there," said Charlton, "Perez said he'd probably move you over to a motel on the west side in Castle Rock. You'll be lodged there for the rest of your work at the Visitor Center. He wants you there for at least a couple of days before Labor Day so that you all can get used to things before the heavy-use weekend. That's one of the agency's newest Visitor Centers and they expect thousands of visitors over the three-day holiday, many from the Portland-Vancouver area; the Seattle-Tacoma-Olympia areas in Washington; and the Salem-Corvallis-Eugene areas in Oregon. You'll be busy, but it should be a lot of fun, too," said Neal.

"Sounds like it," said Kade. "I'm looking forward to it. Any idea on the length of the assignment?"

"Ron said it should last between two and three weeks," Neal replied. "You can work that out with him once you're there. I'll confirm things with your four other team members and get back with all five of you Monday morning about the meeting time with Ron. He'll take care of your hotel and motel arrangements for the entire trip. I'll give you the name of the hotel when I talk with you Monday morning and any other information that you'll need."

"I'm going to ask each one of you to make your own plane reservations to Portland," Charlton continued, "arriving mid to late afternoon on Tuesday, and to take a cab to the hotel in Vancouver. Ron said he'd like to meet with you around 6:00 p.m. their time in the hotel lobby, but I'll have the exact details on Monday. And Ron will be wearing his Forest Service uniform, so you'll be able to recognize him right away. Any other questions?"

"No, I guess that covers it for now," answered Kade. "We can fill in the rest of the blanks when you call Monday morning. Thanks Neal."

"Thank you Kade. We were sure we could count on you," said Neal.

Kade never failed to marvel at the many different types of opportunities and experiences that came his way with the U.S. Forest Service. Sure, there were the day-to-day jobs that sometimes got tiring, but there were many exciting adventures, too.

A couple of times a year it seemed like there were travels to other locations for meetings, training sessions, or temporary work assignments that were always interesting. Many times his wife was able to go with him and they would make a short vacation out of it. However, she wouldn't be able to come along on this Mount St. Helens assignment.

After letting Lynn know what was going on, Kade spent the rest of Friday coordinating things with Dorene and the rest of his District staff. By the time he left for the day, Dorene had already made plane reservations for Tuesday. Kade would meet with all District employees first thing Monday morning and answer any questions they might have. He would also name one of his two top assistants as the Acting Ranger while he was gone.

 On Monday, Kade had learned the names of the other
four people going on the detail with him. They were:
Rusty Elliott from Vermont; Lexi Sustakis from
Michigan; Gary Comey from Pennsylvania; and Jane
Anderson from West Virginia. Kade didn't really know
any of them, although he had met Comey once at a
meeting in Milwaukee. He also knew Anderson's
husband from several years previous when they had
both worked in Minnesota. It should be a good group
with plenty of experience in recreation and visitor
information, Kade thought.

Neal Charlton had also provided the information for
their first night's lodging at the Hilton Vancouver,
which was where Ron Perez would meet them Monday
evening at 6:00 p.m.

Kade's flight Tuesday from Columbus, Ohio to Portland,
Oregon, with connections in Chicago, had gone off
without a hitch. He arrived at the Portland Airport just
after 1:00 p.m. Pacific Coast Time, claimed his baggage,
hailed a cab, and arrived at the Vancouver hotel around
2:30. His room was ready, so he checked in and decided
to take a short nap after calling his wife to let her know
that he had arrived safely. None of the other team
members had arrived yet.

After his nap, Kade grabbed a quick shower, changed
clothes, and went downstairs. Sure enough, there in his

Forest Service uniform was a man Kade assumed was
Ron Perez. He was standing talking with two ladies,
who Kade figured were Jane and Lexi, as well as Gary
Comey, whom he recognized. Introductions were made
and Ron suggested they move to the hotel restaurant
where he had a table reservation, while waiting for
Elliott to arrive.

They got a table where they had a good view out to the
lobby. Ron made a quick call and learned that Elliott's
flight had been delayed in Denver and he wouldn't be
arriving for a few hours.

While they ate, Ron gave them an overview of the
Gifford Pinchot National Forest and explained what to
expect over the next couple of weeks. There were still a
few blanks to fill in, but starting tomorrow they would
drive over to Cougar in a Forest Service van that had
been dropped off in the parking lot earlier that day. It
would be the team's vehicle for the next couple of
weeks.

Ron would meet them at the Spruce Pine Motel at 9:30
a.m. on Wednesday morning in Cougar, about an hour's
drive from Vancouver. The motel was a small rustic
facility with cabins. Ron reserved a two bedroom cabin
for Lexi and Jane; another two bedroom cabin for Rusty
and Gary; and a smaller cabin for Kade.

After answering a few questions, Ron left to go home, while the team members stayed for a while and got to know each other a little better. Kade felt really good about the quality of the members of this team. The group decided to meet for breakfast the next morning before heading out to Cougar. On his way to his room, Kade left word at the front desk for Rusty Elliott to meet them the next morning in the restaurant at 7:00 a.m.

At breakfast on Wednesday morning, the team briefed Elliott on Perez' comments from the previous evening. They also heard about Rusty's three-hour stay at the Denver Airport, while mechanics fixed a problem with the plane he was taking to Portland.

Shortly after 8:00 a.m., the team was packed and loaded in the van and on their way to the Spruce Pine Motel in Cougar.

When they arrived about an hour later, there was Ron Perez waiting for them in the parking lot. Kade could already tell that this assignment was well-planned and organized. If there was anything that Kade liked, it was a well-planned operation. A quick glance around the facility impressed Kade. It was very well maintained, with several rustic cabins located along a winding circle road. The office was located at the entrance, on one side of the parking lot.

After Rusty introduced himself to Perez, the group convened to a small meeting room just off the lobby of the motel. Ron knew the motel manager and had previously explained to him what this group would be doing. Ron had an armful of maps and various papers and he asked Kade to carry a small box, too.

Once they were all seated at a large circular table, Ron gave each person a folder with information and he spread out a large Gifford Pinchot National Forest map. He began to explain where they were located on the map, key roads and landmarks, and the layout of the Mount St. Helens National Volcanic Monument, where the team would be focusing most of its efforts for the next couple of weeks. He also showed the team the location of some of the Forest's popular recreation sites, which they would be asked to visit and to make any suggestions they might have for improvements.

Ron said that although the team would be required to submit a report about their findings and recommendations, there would be ample time over the next few days during their drives around the Forest to enjoy the sights and almost become tourists. None of the team members had visited this area before, so they were all glad that it wouldn't be "nose to the grindstone" non-stop work for this entire assignment.

The Mount St. Helens Assignment

It was now 1988, over eight years since the devastating eruption of Mount St. Helens on May 18, 1980. Ron explained how recreation and visitor information facilities had been developed since then. President Carter had visited the area soon after the eruption and declared it a disaster area, which had allowed federal funds to flow into a four-county area, both for federal purposes and for recovery needs of citizens and local governments.

In August of 1982 President Reagan signed into law a measure that set aside 110,000 acres of the Gifford Pinchot National Forest as the Mount St. Helens National Volcanic Monument. It was set up to provide for scientific studies, educational purposes, and recreational opportunities.

Perez told the group that there were over 100 National Monuments in the United States, primarily meant to preserve unique geologic and natural landmarks, as well as important buildings and historical areas. The buildings and structures included places like Fort Matanzas near St. Augustine, Florida, a Spanish fortress, which guarded the oldest European settlement in the United States. It also included the Statue of Liberty in the New York City harbor.

Areas of giant sequoia trees in California were also set aside as National Monuments, as well as Devils Tower, a large, unique rock of volcanic origin over 1,200 feet high in Wyoming. Devils Tower was the first declared National Monument, established by President Teddy Roosevelt in 1906.

Ron Perez went on to explain that most National Monuments were managed by the National Park Service and the Bureau of Land Management, although there were a few managed by the U.S. Forest Service and other federal agencies. And he said that the Forest Service was committed to making the Mount St. Helens monument one of the nation's very best. That's where this team's assignment would fit in: By providing a fresh set of eyes and ideas on how to continue the development of the recreational portion of the monument. And they were also expected to work at the Visitor Center over the Labor Day holiday.

The scientific studies were coordinated by another person in the Supervisor's Office, Ron explained, with help from the Regional Office in Portland, as well as several universities. These studies already numbered over 400 and included volcanic studies, as well as forestry, soils, wildlife, fisheries, and numerous other scholarly pursuits.

Ron said he had arranged for a District Forester to take the team behind some locked gates one day next week to view a few of the study sites, as well as to see areas that were being left to recover naturally. He thought they might even be able to walk down to what was left of the old Spirit Lake, or actually what was now the "new" Spirit Lake, and see many of the floating trees which had been left that way following the eruption eight years previous.

Ron reminded the team that Harry Truman, the cantankerous old owner of a lodge at Spirit Lake, was now buried 150 feet or more below the ground following the landslides and mudflows that resulted from the volcanic eruption. Kade remembered hearing about how Truman had refused to evacuate the area in 1980 and he became quite the "folk hero" to many folks after his stubbornness was highlighted by national media.

As far as the educational component of the monument's mission, much of that would continue to evolve over the years with the results of the scientific studies. But Perez also explained the educational outreach being done by staff at the District Offices, as well as the Supervisors Office. Much of this included presentations to school groups, guided hikes and tours, development of educational brochures and pamphlets, and, of course, activities focused at the Visitor Center, where Kade's team would spend several days during the latter part of their detail.

By the time Ron had finished explaining what the group's assignment would be for the next several days, it was nearly lunchtime and he had to leave for an afternoon meeting back in Vancouver. He gave Kade his contact information, as well as that of the Monument Manager in Amboy, including their home phone numbers in case those were needed for any reason.

Ron told Kade that the Monument Manager expected to meet with them at his office on Friday morning at 9:00 a.m. He explained that the title "Monument Manager" was equal to that of a District Ranger, but that obviously there were different management duties than a normal Forest Service Ranger District.

They said their goodbye's and Ron said he would meet them here in Cougar again at 9:30 a.m. on Monday, unless he heard otherwise. The team decided to eat lunch and then map out their strategy and agenda for the next few days.

What a unique opportunity this assignment was. There would be plenty of hard work, for sure, including working during the weekends, but it would be an exciting experience, too.

After lunch, Kade asked each member of the team what they expected to learn from this assignment and also what they thought they could contribute to the Gifford Pinchot National Forest.

"How about we start with you, Jane; what are your expectations?" Kade asked.

"Well, as you know Kade, I work as an Interpretive Specialist at the Cranberry Visitor Center on the Monongahela National Forest," Jane Anderson began. "I've been there several years now and I have a good idea of what works and what doesn't work when it comes to managing a visitor center, at least in the Eastern Forest Service Region. I should be able to offer suggestions to the staff at the Mount St. Helens Visitor Center. Plus, I expect to learn new things from the folks out here. I've heard a lot of good things about this brand new Forest Service visitor center," Jane concluded.

"Oh, by the way," Jane continued, "my husband said to say hello."

"Say hi to Jimmy, too," said Kade. "He and I both worked on the Superior National Forest in Minnesota for a couple of years. I guess that was before you met him. I'll have to tell you some stories," Kade said jokingly.

"Please do," Jane replied.

"Only kidding, Jane; only kidding. I've nothing but good things to say about Jimmy Anderson," Kade said.

"How about you, Gary?" Kade said to Comey.

"Being a Landscape Architect, I've been involved with campground construction and improvements on the Allegheny National Forest, as well as hiking trail layout and sign locations," said Gary Comey. "Also, I assist with timber sale design from the visual standpoint, trying to help minimize any negative aesthetic concerns that may arise from timber harvests."

"Anytime I visit new national forests, I get ideas for all of those things," Comey continued. "I'll also be looking for anything helpful in those areas that I can share with the Gifford Pinchot folks."

"Very good, Gary. How about you, Lexi? Would you share your thoughts about this assignment?" Kade asked Sustakis.

"Currently, I handle the office management for our Ranger District in Michigan. I supervise two permanent and two temporary employees," explained Lexi. "I also serve as the Good Host coordinator, working with employees to make sure we do a good job with visitor information. I'll offer suggestions to personnel out here, if I see any areas that need improvement," continued Sustakis, "but actually I expect to learn a lot and be able to take home new ideas."

"Thanks Lexi," said Kade. "And how about you, Rusty?"

"I've done just about everything that a Recreation Technician is responsible for, whether it involves developed campgrounds, remote camping, trails, picnic areas, and even wilderness patrols," explained Elliott. "I've done maintenance, cleanup, repairs, built picnic tables and bulletin boards. I am certified as a law enforcement officer, too" Rusty went on. "For the past two years, I've been heavily involved with summer crews, youth groups, and volunteer organizations in completing a thorough trail inventory and repair project for over 30 miles of hiking trails on our District of the Green Mountain National Forest."

"I'm sure I'll see things here that will help me do a better job back home," continued Rusty. "I will also make suggestions, if I see places where these Washington employees can improve their management of the national forest."

"Oh, and one other thing, Kade," said Rusty. "I want to learn as much as I can about Bigfoot, or Sasquatch, while I'm here. It's my understanding that this area is one of the places in the country that reports the most Bigfoot sightings. Maybe we'll even see one."

"O-kay-ay," replied Kade hesitatingly, as he noticed the other team members looking at one another. "Maybe we can work out something on that."

Kade went on to give the team his background in visitor center management, recreation work he had been involved with, and his experience in public relations. He told the group about the weekly newspaper columns he had been writing for a few years, which focused on various outdoor and natural resource topics, as well as Forest Service items of interest and concern to local readers in his area.

"That's good," said Rusty. "You can write the final report. That's not my strong point."

"We will all contribute to the final report," said Kade. "We certainly have a well-rounded and experienced team. I'm looking forward to working with all of you for the next couple of weeks."

Following that short discussion, the team talked about the assignments that Perez had given them, to make sure they were all in agreement as to what they were expected to accomplish. Initial tasks included driving the roads located south and east of the mountain to get a general idea of the various sites; a trip out to the Windy Ridge Viewpoint, which was the closest view into the volcano blast area, to sit in on a presentation by a Forest Service Interpretive Specialist; and then to continue north and visit a couple of the campgrounds managed by the adjacent Ranger District near Randle.

Finally, they were to spend a couple of days at the Climbers Bivouac, not far from Cougar on the south side of Mount St. Helens. One of those days would be an actual climb to the crater, while the other day would be spent evaluating parking, signing, trail markings, safety concerns, and talking with hikers.

The Forest was evaluating several things there, including limiting the number of hikers each day, instituting a permit system, and other considerations. For each one of the assignments, Ron expected a write-up with observations, recommendations, and any other information the team felt would be helpful to the Forest managers.

Since they had to meet with the Monument Manager on Friday morning, the team decided that day would also be best to visit Windy Ridge in the afternoon.

Ron had suggested they do the two-day hikers/climbing evaluation on the weekend, when use was heaviest.

Tomorrow they would drive as many of the roads on the east side as possible, getting a good overall feel for that side of the monument and surrounding areas.

That would leave Monday to visit and evaluate a couple of the campgrounds. The team would work on their reports Tuesday. Kade would call Perez and have him meet the team on Tuesday morning instead of Monday morning.

After the team had laid out its plans for the next six days, they spent the rest of Wednesday afternoon reading through the information packets and studying the maps that Ron had left with them. It was going to be fun, but there was a lot of hard work in front of them, too. Plus, it didn't even include the second part of their assignment, which was working at the Visitor Center.

After breakfast on Thursday morning, the group piled into the van for a day of driving and getting a feel for what the Gifford Pinchot National Forest looked like. Kade was the driver. He was prone to feeling queasy if he rode in the back seat of a van and none of the others wanted to drive anyway.

It was nearly 70 miles from Cougar to Randle and they would make that round trip today with numerous stops and drives down side roads, too. They had been told that there were three or four restaurants in Randle, so they would plan on being there for lunch.

Randle was a small community with just over 1,000 in population, but in contrast to Cougar's 100 or so people, it would seem like a city. They could also fill up the van with gas in Randle; they didn't want to run out of gas on any of the back roads.

The scenery was stunning, whether looking toward the Mount St. Helens volcano itself or toward the east with the prominent feature being Mount Adams, the second highest mountain in the state of Washington. That mountain rose to 12,280 feet and was situated along the eastern boundary of the Gifford Pinchot National Forest. Like Mount St. Helens (which was now about 8,300 feet in elevation and pre-blast was about 9,600 feet), Mount Adams was considered a potentially active volcano, although it had been dormant for over 1,000 years.

That part of the Forest to the east was managed from the District Ranger's Office in Trout Lake, which was about 50-60 miles from Cougar. On their drive north today, at their nearest point they would only be 25-30 miles from Mount Adams.

They had learned from some of the information that Ron Perez had given them that on the southern flank of the mountain stood the 200-foot tall 'Big Tree', one of the largest known ponderosa pines in the world. It was reportedly over seven feet in diameter.

Other tree species in the area included conifers like Douglas fir, silver fir, western hemlock, noble fir, western red cedar, and lodgepole pine, among others, as well as a few hardwoods such as bigleaf maple and alder. This was in quite a contrast to the oak-hickory and northern hardwood forests of the east that Kade was used to.

It was also interesting to note that trees did not grow above a certain elevation on the mountains. This "tree-line" appeared to Kade to be between 5,000 and 6,000 feet, or maybe even higher in some areas. Above this there were rock formations and at the highest points there was snow cover and glaciers, even now in late August. Quite different than Ohio!

The trip to Randle took them across or adjacent to several creeks and streams. Kade loved to fish and he wished there was time to try to catch some of the trout that he had read about in the information packet – bull trout, rainbows, cutthroat, brown trout and brookies. Maybe he could get back here someday on a true vacation and do a little fishing.

The entire team was quite impressed with the scenery

and at several vantage points they could see the large and imposing snow covered mountain to the north, Mount Ranier, rising to 14,410 feet in elevation. It was the highest point in the entire northwest. The area around Mount Ranier, which was just north of the Gifford Pinchot National Forest, was designated as a National Park in 1899, one of the oldest ones in the country.

It was also an active volcano and labeled as one of the 16 most dangerous volcanoes in the world, due primarily to its close proximity (just over 50 miles) to the Olympia-Tacoma-Seattle areas. The most recent smaller eruptions had occurred in the late 1800s. From the town of Randle to Mount Ranier in a straight line was probably only 25-30 miles.

Of course, as the team members had flown into Portland, they passed very close to Mount Hood and could see it clearly. It was located about 50 miles east of Portland at an elevation of about 11,240 feet. It, too, was considered an active volcano and was the highest peak in the state of Oregon.

All of the team agreed that these mountains – Hood, St. Helens, Adams, and Ranier – were beautiful to view, but that it would also kind of give them the creeps to live so close to four active volcanoes. Even though eruptions were not very frequent, they had occurred in the past. Based upon what had happened at Mount St. Helens on May 18, 1980, the next time any of the others erupted, devastation and tragedy would likely occur.

The team had begun their trip that morning, pulling out of the Spruce Pine parking lot at 8:00 a.m. and by the time they returned, it was almost 6:00 p.m. It had been a long, but interesting day with lots of good conversation and wonderful scenery.

The lunch in Randle was very good and they had stopped a number of times to stretch, walk around, and take some photos. It was a good start to their assignment and each person felt like they were now ready to get into more detailed work over the next several days.

After breakfast on Friday morning the team headed for Amboy to meet with the Monument Manager, Kent Dorman, and his staff. As usual, things were well organized and promptly at 9:00 a.m. the team was seated in the conference room. Dorman welcomed the team and introduced several of his staff members.

He gave a short background talk about the Gifford Pinchot National Forest and his Ranger District, which included about 150,000 acres of regular national forest land, as well as an additional 110,000 acres of the national monument. He then covered what he understood to be the team's assignment, which was almost exactly what Ron Perez had explained to them on Wednesday in Cougar.

One of Dorman's assistants presented an excellent and informative 20-minute slide program, questions were answered, and more information packets were distributed to each team member. The assistant mentioned that some of the primary wildlife species in the area included black-tail deer, elk, spotted owls, black bear, cougar, and grouse. There were even a few wild turkeys and lots of trout fishing.

Kade told Dorman that they planned to drive out to Windy Ridge today, making several stops along the way, and then spend the weekend talking with climbers and making the hike to the crater themselves.

Dorman thought this would work out very well. He said that on Monday one of his Foresters, Don Mastick, could accompany them. On the way to visiting the two campgrounds near Randle, they could visit a couple of the forestry research studies that had been established within the Monument boundaries.

Dorman also said there was an active timber sale not far from Randle that they could stop and see. With the Forester accompanying them, he could explain what was going on and answer any questions they might have about timber management on the Gifford Pinchot National Forest.

This national forest reportedly had the second highest timber harvest volume in the nation. Dorman's District had harvested over 13 million board feet of timber in August alone, quite an impressive amount. It was all done with professional forestry management in a careful and sustained manner with the future of the forest in mind.

As a Forester himself, Kade thought that visiting a timber sale was a great idea. After all, timber management was one of the primary multiple-use activities of the Forest Service, along with recreation, watershed protection, wildlife management, and grazing. Dorman said he would call the District Ranger at Randle and clear the timber sale visit with him, since it was located on that adjacent District.

Kent explained that the acreage within the National Monument boundaries was managed as a preservation unit. No active management was taking place like on the other national forest acres. Scientific studies were taking place, over 400 in fact, but the major thrust was to observe the natural recovery of the area affected directly by the eruption.

Dorman then led a half-hour discussion on what to

expect on the weekend with the climb to the crater rim; and also what kinds of information would be helpful for the team to gather for him, including recommendations on how to improve that hiking segment of the Mount St. Helens experience for the public.

Dorman also pointed out some locations on the map where they would want to stop today and spend a few minutes on their trip to Windy Ridge. The last "Ranger Talk" by an Interpretive Specialist was scheduled for 3:00 p.m.

By 10:30 a.m. they were ready to head out for Windy Ridge. Kade was glad they had thought to have the restaurant staff at Spruce Pine prepare sack lunches for them. There wouldn't be enough time to find a restaurant today.

As they were leaving, Dorman also said he would have Mastick meet them Monday morning at the Spruce Pine restaurant for breakfast. Kade thanked Dorman for everything and said he hoped they would meet again someday, perhaps on a fire assignment.

Dorman told Kade that he was originally from back East and had attended forestry school at Purdue University in Indiana. At some point, he said, he would like to head back closer to home to finish up his career.

On his way to the van, Kade thought about some of the differences between his District and this one. This District was about twice the size of his in Ohio, but there were way fewer people living in and around the forest boundaries here. The large acreages created a heavy workload in some ways, but then again, having to deal with fewer people living within the forest boundaries made things a little simpler, too.

There seemed to be more interest in recreation activities here, especially with the high visitor use due to Mount St. Helens. But then again, Dorman didn't have to monitor over 500 oil and gas wells like Kade did back home either.

Also, Kade thought, the boundary lines here were much easier to identify and it was evident where national forest lands were located. Back home, there was private land mixed among the national forest lands and it was not always easy to tell where the boundary lines were. Overall, Kade thought that both locations had their positives and negatives and that managing a Ranger District was just as difficult in one place as another.

So, it was on to Windy Ridge. The drive to the Windy Ridge Road, Forest Service #99, would take about 90 minutes. From there it was 16 miles along a curvy road to the Windy Ridge Viewpoint. Of course, there were several places along the way, either coming or going, where they would want to stop and look around. In any case they would need to be at Windy Ridge no later than 3:00 p.m. for the interpretive presentation by one of the Rangers.

Shortly before Noon the team had turned off Rt. 25 onto the Windy Ridge Road. A few miles later they stopped for lunch at Bear Meadow, where there were picnic tables and primitive restroom facilities.

This location, about 11 miles northeast of the volcano, was where photographers Keith Ronnholm and Gary Rosenquist had shot the famous progression of photos showing the eruption of Mount St. Helens as it was occurring. Kade had seen these on various TV shows and news sites, as well as documentaries, over the years. The two photographers had barely escaped with their lives, although others were not so lucky, as the blast moved rapidly toward them.

Bear Meadow was actually located near the edge of where the blast zone ended, with deflections occurring because of the topography at that location. It provided the tourist some of the first good views directly into the volcano and to see the forest destruction that had occurred.

After a quick lunch break, Kade reminded the team members that this was the day they needed to begin taking good notes for their report – observations, positive and negative impressions, helpful recommendations, and photos. They had done a little of that on their trip Thursday, but today it was time to get serious about their assignment.

With that, they continued their drive out the Windy Ridge Road. They could see above them on the slopes the large trees that had escaped the volcano's blast, but below them trees were scattered about the hillsides. In some areas salvage logging had taken place, but as they got closer to the volcano, trees had been left lying where they had fallen. For the rest of the day, the closer they got to the volcano, the team observed trees that had been blown over and were lying in one direction from the force of the blast. From a distance they resembled match sticks lying on the ground.

The team next stopped at Miner's Car, the flattened, burned, and ash-filled remnants of the Parker family's vehicle, which was tossed over 60 feet during the eruption. The three Parker family members had come to inspect their miner's claim and were staying in a cabin on the nearby claim. They all perished in the blast. The car is fenced off as a testament to the powerful force of the blast and an interpretive sign was erected nearby.

The team then walked to Meta Lake, just a few hundred

feet from the Miner's Car parking lot. When Mount St. Helens erupted, the lake lay beneath eight feet of snow. The snowpack protected small plants, brook trout, insect larvae, and hibernating animals from the lateral blast.

Later that summer, thanks to warming waters and an algae bloom, thousands of western toads and other life emerged from the lake, providing food for predators and hastening the recovery of nature within the blast zone. What an amazing story, Kade thought, and less than 1,000 feet from the tragedy of the miner's car.

It was also interesting to note the healthy young Pacific silver fir trees around Meta Lake. They were small enough in 1980 to be entirely covered by the snowpack, and survived while the taller trees nearby were killed. Since 1980 they had grown and seemed to be flourishing. Kade and the team members discussed this and, as was often the case, they were amazed at the recovery power of nature.

Back in the van, the team drove a couple of miles to the Cascade Peaks Overlook. Along here the road formed the boundary between the designated monument area and the regular national forest zone. It provided quite an interesting contrast in landscapes. On the right side in the monument area, the forest had been left to recover naturally. On the left, downed trees had been salvaged and new trees planted.

The natural recovery zone was definitely lagging behind the growth shown across the road where the trees had been planted. All of the team agreed that this would be an important site for scientists to study and compare recovery methods for many years to come.

Continuing their drive to the Harmony Viewpoint, they were now only about three miles from Windy Ridge Overlook, where the Ranger presentation was scheduled in about an hour.

About 700 feet below the Harmony Overlook was Spirit Lake. Born from an earlier eruption, when debris from Mount St. Helens dammed the Toutle Valley, the lake raised higher when thick pumice deposits were deposited some 400 years ago.

These changes occurred while Native Americans lived in areas surrounding the mountain. Their legends, which told of "evil spirits" inhabiting the lake, are probably based on episodes of sudden drops in lake level that were accompanied by destructive mudflows. Thus, the name - Spirit Lake. This background information was on a handout given to the team members in their packets.

The "spirit" of the lake had periods of beauty and tranquility, too. Many residents of Washington and Oregon had spent happy summer camp days on Spirit Lake at Harmony Falls Resort. The resort was reached by boat and was a haven for people weary of cities and the pace of 20th century life. Canoeing on the pre-1980 lake, surrounded by old growth forests, was a time-trip back to the Northwest of the 1800s.

But that tranquility had disappeared in seconds of unimaginable violence as the giant 1980 eruption and resulting avalanche swept down from Mount St. Helens. Hundreds of feet thick, and moving at express train speeds, the landslide slammed into the lake. When the debris avalanche entered the lake, a giant wave surged 850 feet up the opposite shore. As the wave crashed back down, it swept the already blown-down trees into the lake. The resulting "log mat" covered much of the new lake and it now drifted with the wind on the lake surface.

When the violence had abated, the first witnesses in rescue helicopters could hardly believe their eyes: the lake was a mile longer and 200 feet higher than it had been the day before. Its shores had been swept clean; the surrounding forest was gone and a mat of shattered logs covered the dead lake. Steam explosions still rose from the southwest shoreline as pyroclastic flows continued to sweep down from the crater.

Kade really wanted to take the one-mile hike down to the lakeshore, but there was not time. Plus he was pretty sure from what Kent Dorman had told the group this morning, they would be close to Spirit Lake next week anyway, when the Forester was going to take them to see some research plots near there.

So, it was on to Windy Ridge. Arriving with a few minutes to spare before the last Ranger's talk of the day, the team took a quick restroom break before settling in at the amphitheater for the presentation. Some of the points made by the Ranger included:

- Windy Ridge was 4,170 feet in elevation, and you could look right into the blast area of Mount St. Helens.
- At about four miles distance, this was the closest observation point to the mountain. The team could see the immediate blast zone, the extensive tree damage, the new lava dome forming, and the remnants of the landslides and mudslides which had occurred on May 18, 1980.
- You could also see down to Spirit Lake, which was at 3,445 feet in elevation.
- Nearly everything in view from Windy Ridge was within the area devastated by the 1980 eruption.
- Harry's Ridge is named for Harry Truman, owner of the Spirit Lake Lodge, who was killed when the huge avalanche buried his resort.

Harry, along with his 16 cats (and as many as 15-20 raccoons that he fed), was buried beneath 150 – 200 feet of debris from the mudflow.

- The scar where trees and soil were scoured down to bedrock by the blast and the avalanche can still be seen on Harry's Ridge.
- Beginning in the summer of 1983, visitors have been able to drive to Windy Ridge, on U.S. Forest Service Road 99. From this vantage point overlooking Spirit Lake, people can see firsthand not only the evidence of a volcano's destruction, but also the remarkable, gradual (but faster than originally predicted) recovery of the land as vegetation re-grows and wildlife returns.
- The closest lake to Mount St. Helens and in the direct path of the blast and avalanche, Spirit Lake had suffered the most destruction.
- Besides being choked by avalanche debris, ash, and countless tons of organic material, the temperature of the water was superheated when pyroclastic flows poured into the lake. No life was thought to have survived.
- Spirit Lake went through the same drastic chemical changes that the smaller lakes did, but on such a large scale that some people doubted that it could ever support life again. Within five years, though, recovery of the water chemistry was almost complete. The addition of huge amounts of fresh water by rain and melting

snow, and the stirring action of wind and waves
adding oxygen, were two of the most important
factors. Spirit Lake now supported a wide variety
of aquatic life.

- The mats of logs now floating on the lake at first
covered nearly its entire surface. Some sink every
year, but most will float for many years. The log
mats move across the water, nudged by the wind,
changing the look of the lake every day.
- Did the volcano blow its top? Not really. Most of
the summit slid away in the avalanche, and the
resulting crater was enlarged by the blast and
high ash cloud eruption that followed. About
90% of the missing mountain was contained in
the avalanche debris.

After the excellent presentation by the Interpretive
Specialist, the team decided to climb the 368 steps to an
adjacent observation area for a better view of
everything. To a person, each team member wanted to
go down to Spirit Lake and they hoped that would be
possible on Monday.

Kade thought to himself, too, that he wanted to learn
more about Harry Truman. That whole story intrigued
him.

It was now 4:30 p.m. and the team was tired. They were
all ready to head back to the restaurant at the Spruce
Pine Motel, eat a bite, and get ready for their weekend

climbing adventures. They decided they would meet for breakfast Saturday morning to go over their notes from Friday's trip and to plan their day.

As they ate breakfast on Saturday and went over their notes from the previous day, Kade could tell that this group was very observant and was going to help him put together a very good report.

True to his background in landscape architecture, Gary Comey already had some helpful suggestions about improvements in layout and design of parking areas; Jane Anderson had written down some items for the Gifford Pinchot personnel to consider about interpretive talks and presentations; Lexi Sustakis had made several notes concerning signs, including both wording and sign locations; and Rusty Elliott had some ideas about trails, both existing ones and potential new ones.

The team had to decide which day to hike the Monitor Ridge hiking route to the volcano's summit and which day to talk with visitors and evaluate the trail itself. Based upon weather predictions, either day would be fine for the hike.

"Let's hike it both days," suggested Elliott. "We can talk with visitors as we hike."

"I don't know if I can hike it twice," said Lexi. "How long is the hike, anyway?"

"Well, from what Kent Dorman told us and from the information that Ron Perez gave us in the packets, it's about a 5-mile hike one way," said Kade. "And Kent said it should take us about seven or eight hours round trip, counting rest stops. From the Climbers Bivouac parking lot, the first half of the hike is through trees and other forest vegetation. The second half to the crater rim is mostly through lava flow areas, boulders, loose pumice, and ash. I expect the second part of the hike to be pretty tiring and dusty. The footing will be a little slippery too, I suspect," said Kade.

 "Maybe the most difficult part for us "easterners" will be the elevation," Kade continued. "The parking lot where we'll begin the hike is 3,700 feet elevation and the top will be over 8,000 feet. So, the air will be a little "thin" for us. We'll have to take frequent breaks," said Kade. "Plus, it will be pretty steep, especially the last half of the hike above the tree line. Make sure you bring a couple of bottles or canteens of water."

"That settles it for me," said Jane. "One day will be enough for me to hike that kind of terrain, if I can even make it at all."

"I agree," chimed in Gary. "The other day we can take

more time to talk with visitors and hikers. Plus, it will be easier to write down our notes."

"Well, I guess I'm out-voted," said Rusty. "But let's hike it the first day, so we know what we're dealing with. Plus, I need to get some exercise. We've been riding in the van the whole time we've been here."

"That's not a bad idea," Kade said. "If we hike it the first day, we'll have a better understanding of the whole experience and be able to ask visitors more meaningful questions the second day."

The team all agreed, so after grabbing their sack lunches, they all went back to their rooms to make sure they each had the proper clothing and boots for hiking.

The drive out to the Climbers Bivouac was about 12 miles and by 9:00 a.m. they had their back-packs on and were ready to start the climb. This location was the highest elevation where a road was located in the Mount St. Helens area. They would only climb another 1,100 feet in elevation for nearly the first half of the hike and still be below 5,000 feet. From that point on, however, they would be above the timberline and the climb would get much steeper.

"Follow me," said Rusty, as the group began its climb.

"I'm afraid that's what we're going to hear all day long," mumbled Jane to Lexi, who just smiled and nodded. Gary joined in behind the two ladies.

Kade decided to bring up the rear, so he could monitor how things were going and be close to help anyone who stumbled or had an accident.

As they had been told, the first half of the climb was a traditional hiking trail through a tree-lined forest. It was not terribly steep because there were enough switchbacks located along the route to make the climb somewhat gentle in nature. The trail was well maintained with water bars and out-slopes to divert rain water from the tread itself. In just over an hour they had reached the last location where there were toilet facilities, near the edge of the timberline.

"Piece of cake," yelled Elliott, who had reached this location well ahead of the others. "We're almost halfway already."

"Just remember, Rusty, that the second part of the hike is much steeper and the footing will be difficult," said Kade.

"Yeah, but it's mostly a straight shot from here," said Elliott. "I don't think this is going to take us nearly as long as they told us."

Lexi, who was already a little winded, looked this time at Jane and said, "Sometimes I just want to smack him."

"Let's take a 10-minute break," said Kade, "to water-up and use the restrooms before we start the second half of the hike."

Once they were all ready to go again, Kade reminded them of the boulders, loose rocks, and ash that they would have to hike through. And since Rusty would again go in the lead, Kade reminded him to follow the posts that were located along the way to keep people on the trail.

"No sweat," said Elliott, "I could do this hike with my eyes closed."

The two ladies rolled their eyes at one another, while Comey just smiled and suppressed a laugh.

After breaking out above the timberline, the hike did indeed get steeper, as the team made its way through quite a distance of blocky lava flow material and volcanic boulders. The going got slower due to the steepness, the terrain, and the increase in elevation. Rest stops were more frequent, even for Elliott, as they neared the last post marker at about 7,000 feet in elevation.

It was now just after noon and time for lunch and a rest break, Kade told the team. It had taken them about twice as long to cover approximately the same distance as it had the first part of their hike.

"This is as far as I'm going," Gary Comey announced. "I can see the top from here and I've seen photos of the crater. That's all I need. After we eat, I'm going to go right back down to that last big boulder we passed, settle in for a nap on the shady side, and wait till you guys come by on the way back down. That is, if none of you die. Nothing but loose rocks and dust from here on up anyway. I'm done!"

"Not me," said Jane. "I'm getting to the top if I have to crawl the last 100 yards on bloody knees and fingers."

"Me, too," said Lexi. "If Jane can do it, so can I."

"Well, I came to climb this mountain and look down into the eye of that volcano. And that's what I intend to do," Kade said, as Rusty nodded in approval.

After they ate their lunch, Kade checked to make sure each climber had at least half of their water left. Thankfully, the restaurant staff had included a can of iced tea in each sack lunch, too. Kade also reminded them that once they got close to the rim of the crater to be very careful, even though the rim path was said to be several feet wide in places. They had been told that it was not unheard of for chunks of the rim to break loose and fall inward toward the crater.

"Let's get going," Kade said. "We have less than half a mile to go. I'd like to get there before 2:00 p.m."

"And I'd like to get there before tomorrow, the rate we're going," wisecracked Rusty. Then he let out a big laugh to let the team know he was just kidding before any of them could get mad at him.

As Gary made his way back down to the large boulder, the team began its final ascent. And sure enough, the footing was bad – small loose rocks, pumice, and ash. It was often one step forward and two steps back as they slid all over the place. In fact, Rusty seemed to slide backward more than anyone. As they neared the crater rim, he had a rather long backward slide and both Jane and Lexi reached the summit before Elliott. This amused Kade, observing them from below, but he didn't say anything.

"I won!" Jane yelled, much to Elliott's chagrin.

"And I came in second," shouted Lexi. A red-face Elliott got to the rim next with Kade several feet behind. Kade glanced at his watch and noticed that it was now 1:50 p.m.

The sight was something to behold – the scenery made

117

you think you were on top of the world. That is, until you turned and saw the towering Mt. Adams to the east and the snow covered Mount Ranier in the distance to the north. In the foreground, toward the Mount Ranier view, was Spirit Lake. And they could clearly see the logs floating on the surface.

There was steam coming from fissures down in the lava dome. But Kade noticed that even if someone fell from the rim, they wouldn't come close to landing near the dome. Still, it would be difficult, if not impossible, to climb back to the rim without some assistance.

After about 20 minutes on top, the team was ready to head back down. The first several hundred feet was practically a "butt-slide," but as they neared the first trail post, they were able to walk almost normally. A short distance beyond that point, they came to the first large boulder and, sure enough, there was Comey, seemingly half asleep.

"What time is it?" asked Gary, looking up. "Or should I say what day is it?"

"Very funny," said Elliott. "You sure missed a good view."

"I was the first one to reach the top," said Anderson.

"And I was second," chimed in Lexi.

"So the gals beat you, Rusty?" asked Comey. "Doesn't surprise me any. Your feet are too big and clumsy," Gary laughed.

"Settle down everyone," Kade interjected, just before Elliott was about to say something else back to Comey. "This is all in good fun. But now it's 3:00 o'clock and we need to get back at a decent time in order to wash up and eat."

"Sounds good," said Rusty. "Follow me."

The rest of the team looked at one another and smiled. They fell in behind Elliott, with Kade again bringing up the rear. As they got back near the timberline, they stopped for a short water and restroom break before taking the rest of the normal hiking trail through the woods and back to the parking lot.

By the time they unloaded their backpacks and got into the van, it was 5:30 p.m. The round-trip hike had taken them a little over eight hours, not bad for rookies, who weren't used to the terrain nor the elevation.

During dinner they decided to meet once again the next morning for breakfast and discuss their strategy for talking with trail hikers for that day. This team, Kade observed, was beginning to settle in and have good camaraderie.

At dinner they joked and laughed about Rusty sliding down the upper portion of the trail, about Jane reaching the crater rim first, and about Gary deciding he had had enough hiking and just wanting to take a nap while the rest of the team continued on to view the volcano. Rusty was in good spirits and everyone was getting along great. Kade was glad he had taken this assignment.

The team members all had a big breakfast on Sunday morning and to a person they each said they had been so tired the night before that they slept like babies. That hike to the top of the volcano had completely worn them out. After breakfast, their plan was to drive back out to the Climbers Bivouac and interview hikers. And, once again, the restaurant packed sack lunches for the team.

For those forest visitors starting their hikes, the team would ask questions like:

- Is this your first time taking this hike?
- What are your expectations?
- Where are you from?
- How many in your group?
- How much do you know about Mount St. Helens?
- Where did you get your information about this climb up the mountain?

- Do you know what to expect on this trail – loose rocks, ash, boulders, steepness, etc.?
- And anything else that came up during the interview.

For those coming back down from the summit, the team would ask:

- How was your hike?
- How long did the round trip take?
- Did you run into anything unexpected?
- Was the hiking difficulty what you had anticipated?
- Was the signage adequate? How about the trail posts?
- Any safety concerns that you encountered?
- Did you talk with other hikers along the trail?
- What suggestions do you have to improve the experience?
- Would you do this again, or recommend it to others?
- And anything else that came up during the interview.

Each team member carried a notebook and pens with them. They wrote the questions down so they would have some consistency with what they asked the hikers. Kade reminded them all to wear their Forest Service uniforms that day, so that forest visitors would know they were "official" and not just some random people asking prying questions.

Once the team arrived at the Climbers Bivouac, they decided that Kade, Lexi, and Gary would remain at that location to talk with hikers both coming and going. Rusty and Jane would hike back up to the restroom area near the edge of the timberline and talk with hikers there. Maybe they would even proceed on up the open part of the trail and talk with some hikers along that section, too.

This day was kind of "laid-back" compared to the tiring hike of the previous day, but, still, the team stayed busy asking questions, taking notes, and recording comments. There had been over 50 hikers that day, enough to get a good sampling of opinions and suggestions.

After lunch, Kade had walked up to where Rusty and Jane were working and told them to meet the rest of the team in the parking lot around 4:00 p.m. and they would then call it a day. Monday would be another long day with the District Forester accompanying them to view a timber sale and the visit to two campgrounds.

On Monday morning the team had breakfast with Forester Don Mastick. He said it was about an hour and a half drive to the timber sale location, which he suggested should be the first stop.

It was an active timber operation and was quite impressive. Kade had seen postcards back at the motel that showed a log truck hauling just one huge log – and it had taken up all the space on the trailer. He wondered if they would see any logs that size today. They did not, but a couple of the loaded trucks could only fit three Douglas fir logs on the bed before heading to the mill. Even that was quite impressive to the team! Back home, there were often 15 or 20 logs on a truck, and Kade had never seen fewer than about 10, even of the largest oaks or maples in the woods.

This had indeed been a good stop. Mastick explained the silvicultural considerations in having the timber sale located in that specific area and what kinds of precautions had been taken to minimize erosion and avoid sedimentation of the streams. He explained what types of treatments would be necessary after the logging was completed to ensure adequate site restoration and revegetation of the area. Don also explained the benefits of the timber sale operation to the local economy and answered any questions the team had.

They then piled back in the van and headed to a campground that was not far from Randle. Gary Comey was particularly interested in this stop. It was an older campground, quite scenic and well laid out, as it was tucked neatly into a cove at the base of a small mountain. But Mastick said it was on the Forest's list to be upgraded and renovated in the next couple of years.

Kent Dorman had reminded him to tell the team to offer constructive comments that would help the Forest's recreation staff in their planning efforts.

Comey noted that there were no electric or water hook-ups at the campsites. Water had to be carried from centrally located spigots. There were restrooms with wash basins, but no showers. Also, many of the camping pads could only accommodate tents with a car parked alongside; not big enough for modern pop-up campers or larger trailers.

This campground had certainly been good enough in past years, but was not what modern campers expected. To increase use in the future, some upgrades were definitely in order, Comey said. Those preferring a more primitive camping experience had many other places on the Forest where they could go.

Gary also had some ideas about how to re-locate the campground entrance to eliminate a dangerous situation when turning in from the main road, as well as some suggestions about how to re-configure the two camping loops themselves. He said he would write-up all of his ideas for the final report. Jane, Lexi, and Rusty also had ideas about signs, bulletin boards, garbage containers, and other campground specifics.

It was now lunch time. They were close to a diner just on the edge of Randle and so they headed there for burgers, hot dogs, fries, soft drinks, milkshakes, and so forth. Three days of sack lunches had put them in the mood for this.

It was a great meal, but they were all amazed when Rusty ate two hamburgers, two hot dogs, an order of fries, and drank a soda with one refill. And he got a chocolate milkshake to go! Lexi said he ate like a Sasquatch. The group all had a good laugh about that.

As they headed back south toward the turnoff to Windy Ridge, the team pulled into another campground and took notes once again. This campground was more modern than the previous one, but there were still a number of things that this group of "outside eyes" could offer suggestions on how to improve.

They noted where improvements could be made for parking, signs, access to a picnic pavilion, a short nature trail, and a few other things. What a good group, Kade thought, feeling confident that their final report would be professional and useful to the Gifford Pinchot National Forest.

Leaving the second campground and turning out the road to Windy Ridge, Don asked Kade to pull off where there was a locked gate. A dirt road took off to the west, where Mastick said there were some research studies being done. Only authorized vehicles could drive to those sites. He suggested to Kade that he drive the van from that point on. Kade was a little hesitant, but agreed.

Mastick drove a little too fast, but Kade didn't say anything. He figured Don knew the roads better than he did. Still, Kade was a little nervous in a couple of spots where there were steeper drop-offs and he thought he felt the tires skid slightly. The other team members were pretty quiet and a quick look around told Kade that they were a little frightened, too.

"How often do you drive these roads," Kade asked Mastick.

"At least once a week in good weather," he replied. "Sometimes more often. Don't worry, I know every turn and bump on this road," Mastick replied, sensing some uneasiness on Kade's part.

Pulling into a wide spot for their first stop, Kade and the team breathed a sigh of relief. Safe at last! Kade walked over to Mastick and said that he thought it would be best if he drove from here on out. Don said that he knew the roads better and was used to driving on them, but he reluctantly agreed to let Kade drive from that point on.

"By the way," Kade asked Mastick, "where did you go to Forestry School?"

"Colorado State," he replied, "but I'm originally from West Virginia."

"West Virginia!" Kade shouted. "That's where I'm from. No wonder you can drive these mountain roads so fast."

"I thought Kent said you were from Ohio?" said Mastick.

"That's where I work now, but I grew up in West Virginia and went to Forestry School at West Virginia University in Morgantown," Kade said. "Why did you go to Colorado State and how did you end up out here in Washington?"

"Well, I grew up in Greenbrier County, West Virginia, close to Lewisburg. But I just wanted to go to college out of state," Mastick explained. "I was always interested in the outdoors, and our family had taken a vacation out west when I was about thirteen years old. I was amazed with the scenery in Rocky Mountain National Park, so Colorado State seemed like a good place to go to school. My parents were fine with it," he continued. "At first, I was interested in studying Parks and Recreation, but after two years of college I decided to major in Forest Management."

"I worked for two summers with the Forest Service here in Washington," Mastick continued, "and just fell in love with the northwest. After graduation, they offered me a job on the Gifford Pinchot National Forest and the rest is history. I've been here four years now. I married a local girl from Longview and we hope to stay in the area."

"And by the way," Mastick laughed, "I don't drive these roads too fast!"

"I knew a Jennings from Greenbrier County, West Virginia, when I was in Forestry School," said Kade. "Ever hear of anyone with that name?"

"None that I know of in Lewisburg," replied Mastick. "My grandmother was a Jennings, but her people were all from Raleigh County, near Beckley."

"Well, it's good to meet another West Virginian out here," Kade said. "But I guess I'll still drive the van the rest of the day."

"Oh, by the way," Mastick continued, "we're standing not too far from where a famous West Virginian is buried."

"Who? And where?" Kade asked.

"Harry Truman, the Spirit Lake Lodge owner who refused to evacuate from Mount St. Helens before the volcano erupted," Mastick explained. "And he's now buried about 200 feet deep, not far from here. Or at least that's what everyone thinks. He was never heard from again after the eruption and the mudslides. So, it's a good bet he's buried down there somewhere. And from what he told everyone, that's the way he would've wanted it."

"Truman was from West Virginia?" Kade asked. "I assumed he was a native to this area."

"No, his dad was a logger in West Virginia and he moved the family to Washington in the early 1900s to continue logging out here when Harry was about ten or eleven years old," explained Mastick. "Harry logged for a while, too, I've been told. I don't know too much more, but when you get over to the Visitor Center in a few days, they can tell you more. They have a lot of information about Harry Truman," said Mastick. "They even give a presentation about once a day on Harry Truman. He's become even more famous since he died. People are fascinated about him because of the news coverage he got when he refused to leave his lodge."

"I'll definitely check that out when we work at the Visitor Center," said Kade. "His story has already interested me, but now that I know he was originally from West Virginia, I'm even more interested."

"Let's hear about some of the research studies that are being done in this area," said Kade.

For the next hour and a half, Mastick explained to the team several studies taking place at the National Volcanic Monument. They visited a few of the sites, with Kade now driving, of course; and Don pointed out other studies in the distance that they couldn't drive to. There were research projects monitoring natural recovery; growth studies of trees planted after the volcano; water quality and soil studies; wildlife research; several biological studies focusing on insects, fish, invertebrates, flowers, and emerging plant life; and, of course, numerous studies by geologists and volcano research specialists.

The team was surprised to learn that many larger mammals, especially elk and deer, were fairly abundant in the area once again and, in fact, had begun returning to the area just a couple of years after the eruption, as plant life began to take hold.

Of course, everywhere they looked there were the trees and logs lying on the ground. The ones nearer the blast zone were all knocked down in a straight line by the sheer force of the blast. Others were more scattered about.

Kade mentioned to Mastick that the team wanted to walk down to Spirit Lake, if possible. So, at the closest point to the lake, they parked the van and walked a short distance to Spirit Lake. What an amazing site to see - all of the floating logs on the water, thousands of them.

The team asked Mastick if they could take any of the ash, pumice, or pieces of wood with them. He said, no, but that there was a small pile of these things out near the gate where they had entered the research area. They could grab a couple of items from that pile on their way out. The group had been taking many photos, so they had several of the empty plastic film containers with them. At the gate each person filled a container with ash, grabbed a couple of small pieces of pumice, and took a small piece of wood from a downed tree which had been broken apart when the road had been put in a few years previous. These would be the souvenirs from Mount St. Helens that they would show their friends and families back home.

By the time the group got back to the Spruce Pine motel, it was 5:30 p.m. They said their goodbyes to Don Mastick and thanked him for an informative and interesting day. At dinner the team decided to once again meet for breakfast the next morning – Tuesday - and begin planning the write-up for this first part of their assignment. Ron Perez was going to meet them at 9:30 a.m. They could work on their report most of the day after that.

From what Perez had told Kade on the phone the other evening, he would put them up at a motel in Castle

Rock starting Tuesday evening for the remainder of their detail to the Visitor Center. Castle Rock was over on the west side of Mount St. Helens, a little over an hour from Cougar.

After breakfast on Tuesday morning, the team checked out of their rooms and moved their belongings to the conference room, where the motel owner said they could spend the day working on reports. They were working around the conference table when Ron arrived.

Kade briefed him on the events of the past five days. Perez asked several questions and each team member jumped in to explain various parts of their work so far. Perez seemed very pleased with how things were going.

"Great job so far, guys," Ron told the group. "Keep it up for the rest of your detail here and we will be more than grateful for your help. I know you're working hard and putting in some long days, but hopefully you're having fun, too. I may even give each of you a souvenir coffee mug, if you continue doing so well," Perez joked.

"How about a hat that says 'Bigfoot' on it?" asked Rusty.

"Maybe that, too," grinned Perez.

"I have to stop over in Amboy for a meeting and then get back to the office this afternoon," Perez continued. "I'll leave you alone to work on your draft report the rest of the day. Kade has the information for your motel in Castle Rock. I told them you'd be there by 6:00 p.m. this evening. There's a restaurant across the parking lot that's open until 9:00."

"I'll meet you tomorrow morning in the motel lobby and take you out to the Visitor Center," said Perez. "I'll introduce you to the folks there. You'll get an orientation and then can spend the rest of the day browsing around, looking at the exhibits, and reading background information. Starting Thursday morning, you'll be working there for a few days assisting the regular staff with normal duties."

"The Labor Day holiday is next Monday," Perez explained, "so this coming three-day weekend will be very busy at the Visitor Center. They will really need your help then. Several of their regular employees are still gone on fire details, so they're short-handed that's for sure. Any questions?"

"How long do you think our detail will last?" asked Jane.

"Well, I'm not 100 percent sure right now," answered Perez. "Kade and I were talking about this on the phone the other evening. I'd like to keep you here for at least a few days after Labor Day. That way, our regular Visitor Center folks, who have been working extra hard because they are short-handed, can take some time off to rest before you all leave."

"We were told that our assignment would likely be between two and three weeks long," Kade said. "So that fits in with what I was expecting. Next Tuesday would be two weeks from the day we flew out here."

"We can talk with the Visitor Center manager tomorrow and try to nail it down, if possible," said Perez. "Hopefully, you guys can be flexible with us. Any more questions before I leave?"

"I have one," Rusty said. "When do we get to see a Sasquatch?"

The team all looked around and smiled at each other. Perez wasn't sure for a moment how serious Elliott was, until he noticed Kade and Comey smiling at one another.

"Everywhere we go, there are signs and posters and brochures and postcards and everything else with Sasquatch pictures and information," said Elliott. "They even had a "Sasquatch burger" and a "Bigfoot milkshake" at the diner in Randle the other day. I know they're not supposed to be real," continued Rusty, "but I was just wondering."

"Yes, this is one of the primary areas for Bigfoot sightings," said Perez. "They have quite a bit of information about that at the Visitor Center. The staff there gets a lot of questions about Sasquatch, or Bigfoot. You can read up on that tomorrow. Some even say that the last living Bigfoot was killed in the blast of Mount St. Helens. Who knows? But it's an interesting story nonetheless. You'll even see a large 20-foot statue of a Bigfoot in front of a store over near Toutle, not far from the Visitor Center," Perez said.

"I have to leave for my meeting now. See you all tomorrow morning in Castle Rock," said Ron.

With that, the team continued putting together their notes and combining them on a day-by-day basis. They decided this was the best way to do it for the final report. In addition, for the final report there would also be a separate section of suggestions and recommendations, listed by topic: a section for campgrounds, one for the Visitor Center, one for the hiking trail, one concerning signs, and so on.

Lexi volunteered to type up the information on a typewriter she had borrowed from the motel manager, and she would do the same for their Visitor Center notes. Kade would then take these draft write-ups back home, edit them, and combine them into a draft final report. He would send out copies to everyone on the team to review before he mailed a "final-final," as he called it, to Ron Perez.

The team worked until about 3:00 p.m., having stopped for lunch before resuming. They wanted to get to their motel in Castle Rock, check in to their rooms, and relax a bit before dinner. And wouldn't you know it, during lunch Rusty had ordered a Sasquatch burger and a Bigfoot shake. The only problem was that this restaurant didn't offer those items on the menu.

The waitress didn't seem amused when she said, "We don't have those items on the menu, sir."

"Well, they have them at the diner in Randle," said Elliott.

"Doesn't surprise me," said the waitress. "They do a lot of that 'touristy, gimmicky' stuff up there. We aren't into that around Cougar."

"I guess she doesn't believe Bigfoots are real either," Rusty mumbled, to no one in particular. "In that case, just give me two hot dogs, a cheeseburger, an order of onion rings, a coke, and a chocolate milkshake."

"I guess we have found our 'Bigfoot' right here," the waitress said to Kade. "I thought for a moment he was ordering for the whole table." Everyone laughed, but Rusty.

"Very funny," remarked Elliott. "If that doesn't fill me up, I may order another hot dog."

"By the way, Kade, I hope you mention something about Sasquatch in our final report," said Elliott.

"We'll see," said Kade, letting the matter drop without further comment. But he did promise Rusty that they would get a chance to see the Bigfoot statue near Toutle and take some photos. Kade definitely wanted a photo of Rusty standing beside Sasquatch. He also had a surprise for Elliott at their motel in Castle Rock.

Around 4:30 p.m. that afternoon, the team pulled into the parking lot of their new motel in Castle Rock. There it was, in big letters – THE SASQUATCH INN. There were no Bigfoot statues here. They would have to see that in Toutle. But still, Rusty was a happy man.

"Way to go, Kade!" Elliott said enthusiastically. "Now I can say I stayed where Bigfoot lives."

"I think maybe they're related," laughed Comey.

"Probably a long lost cousin," chimed in Sustakis.

"Or an uncle," added Anderson.

"Okay, enough of that guys," said Kade. "Let's check in, unpack, and meet in the lobby in an hour to go to dinner." Everyone agreed. Kade noticed that Rusty had a little extra bounce in his step on the way to their check-in.

Ron had told Kade he would meet them at the motel on Wednesday morning at 8:30 a.m. The Visitor Center opened at 9:00 a.m. and Perez wanted the team there to have an idea of what was involved with opening the facility each morning. It was only a 10 - 15 minute drive from the motel to the Visitor Center.

After breakfast Wednesday morning, Perez met the group a little earlier than planned and by just after 8:30 a.m. they arrived at the Visitor Center. The facility had been open for only a little over a year now and it was an extremely attractive building.

Comey noted the excellent landscaping job, the layout of the parking lots and walkways, and the beautiful front entrance. Anderson, with her background working at the Visitor Center on the Monongahela National Forest in West Virginia, was truly impressed and said she was really looking forward to seeing the exhibits inside.

They followed Ron's vehicle and parked around back in one of the employee spaces. Perez had a key to the back door and when they entered they were enthusiastically met by the Visitor Center supervisor, Mary Frances Evans.

Mary Frances was there with one other employee. They always had at least two employees open in the mornings for safety reasons. She explained that they turned on the lights, checked the restrooms, adjusted the heating/cooling as necessary, turned on the audio-visual equipment, made sure the brochure racks were full, and a number of other things.

They kept the doors locked until 9:00 a.m., when visitors began arriving. The center closed at 5:00 p.m. and two employees would stay until 6:00 to clean up and get as much ready for the next morning as possible. Evans staggered staff hours for the opening and closing so that everyone was there between 9:30 a.m. and 4:30 p.m. There were half hour lunch breaks.

After introductions Evans said, "We are so glad to have you here. We've been shorthanded for several weeks now with our people being out on fire assignments. It seems like most of the west is on fire. We're glad to help out with these forest fire emergencies, but it has certainly put us in a bind at the Visitor Center," she said.

"Luckily, Washington and Oregon have had adequate rainfall this summer and haven't been affected by wildfires as much as other areas in the west. We'll get you up to speed as quickly as we can today," said Evans. "Tomorrow you will be part of our regular crew. Then, beginning Friday comes the busiest four days of the year over the Labor Day holiday. That's when we'll really be glad that you all are here to help us out."

The Visitor Center normally operated with a staff of five to seven on weekdays and up to nine on weekends and holidays, according to Evans. But she said that for the past six weeks they had only had three to five people available to work each day. That's why these five extra employees from "back East" would be so welcome for the next week or so.

After the busy Labor Day weekend, the regular staff could rotate a couple of days off for rest, while Kade and his crew were still there. And by then, hopefully, some of the regular Visitor Center employees would be back from their fire assignments, too.

Shortly after Perez left to return to the Supervisor's Office, Evans took the group on a walk around the facility, both inside and out, giving as much of an explanation of things as she could in a short time frame. After she was finished with the initial briefing, the team members would "pair up" with regular Visitor Center employees for a more detailed look at specific duties.

Evans explained that this center had opened a few years after the 1980 eruption of the mountain and more or less served as a "gateway" to the mountain from the west side. The Visitor Center was about 30 miles from the mountain. The goal of the center was to provide useful information to visitors about the landscape before the eruption, the historical significance of the eruption, and the post-recovery efforts that were ongoing. Visitors could see the western slope of Mount St. Helens from both the center and from the walking trail outside.

The building itself was quite impressive, a combination of rock and wood, with expansive windows allowing views of the towering trees outside. There were high archways and large wooden columns inside. Adequate walkways and plenty of benches for resting were located throughout the facility. Gary Comey had already begun taking notes. A very attractive building indeed!

As Mary Frances continued the tour for the team, she showed them displays that included: a large model of the volcano; life size mannequins; a functioning seismograph with current live feeds from the volcano; photos of the timeline of events leading up to the blast on May 18, 1980; and information about the history, geology, and recovery of the land since the eruption. Jane Anderson was especially interested in the displays and exhibits.

Evans showed them the indoor theater where various programs were offered twice an hour beginning at 10:05 a.m. until 4:35 p.m. These programs included a standard slide show and a film about the eruption; and then also specific programs by interpretive specialists, including one about Harry Truman and one about the legend of Sasquatch, as well as a short history of the local area. Kade wanted to sit in on that Harry Truman presentation for sure.

Lexi Sustakis thought that the theater was excellent. She was also impressed with the information desk just inside the front door where there were numerous brochures available and there was always a person available to answer visitors' questions. A display board with the times of the various theater presentations was mounted above the desk for visitors to easily see.

Evans showed the team where the outdoor, half-mile hiking trail began. This trail allowed visitors to walk along Silver Lake and across a boardwalk where they could view a variety of aquatic plant and animal life, as well as occasional larger animals and migratory waterfowl. At times, if there were enough employees working that day, the center would provide for a specialist to accompany groups on the hike. Rusty, with his background in trail management, was particularly interested in this.

It was now almost 10:00 a.m. and visitors had been arriving steadily for some time now. Today, Evans had scheduled four employees for duty. One would talk with visitors outside and lead trail hikes if the numbers warranted it. Two would work at the information desk, taking turns starting the projectors for the routine

programs in the theater and then answering any
questions immediately following the programs.

Evans herself would walk near the displays, answering
visitor questions, keeping an eye on everything, and
filling in for others as needed. She also would do two
special presentations that day: one about the vegetation
and the forests of the area, and one about the legendary
Harry Truman. The Truman presentation was
scheduled for 1:35 p.m. and Kade made a mental note
to be there for that one.

Evans left it up to Kade about which team members
would initially accompany which regular employees.
She also suggested that they all take at least a short time
to spend at each location so that they would have an
overall feel for the entire operation before the heavy use
holiday began. They could spend the rest of today and
tomorrow familiarizing themselves with all of these
things. Kade agreed.

Kade started the assignments with Rusty working
outside, Lexi and Gary working at the front desk, and
Jane accompanying Mary Frances as she walked among
the exhibits talking with visitors. Kade would spend
time at each location, making sure he was available to
catch the Harry Truman presentation. Also, as time
allowed each person would watch the regularly
scheduled slide and film presentations in the theater.

Evans gave Kade and each member of his team a card with answers to some of the most frequently asked questions from visitors. These included:

- Mount St. Helens was named by British explorer George Vancouver in 1792 for his friend Baron St. Helens, an English diplomat and nobleman. Vancouver also named three other volcanoes – Mounts Baker, Hood, and Ranier.
- The elevation of Mount St. Helens before the eruption was 9,677 feet and afterward it was 8,365 feet.
- The eruptions of 1980, including several smaller ones prior to the great May 18, 1980 blast, were the first ones of the 20th century. History records show eruptions in the 1800s and geologic evidence indicated many eruptions prior to that time. The last 'major' eruption of the mountain before 1980 had been in 1857.
- The May 18, 1980 eruption killed 57 people. The earthquake that triggered the eruption measured 5.1 on the Richter scale.
- The resulting avalanche traveled a distance of 15 miles, with an estimated volume of earth and debris of 0.7 cubic miles.
- The blast itself devastated an area of 230 square miles with a force 500 times greater than the World War II bombing of Hiroshima.

- The ash cloud reached a height of 16 miles. An estimated 490 tons of ash was hurtled over an area the size of West Virginia.
- The pyroclastic flows were hotter than 800 degrees Fahrenheit. Pyroclastic flows are a mixture of superheated gas, rock, ash, and other debris.
- The mudflows carried by the streams and waterways traveled a distance of 75 miles.
- The crater itself was over one mile wide and 2,000 feet deep.
- At least five smaller explosions occurred later on throughout 1980.
- Trees were blown down as far as 19 miles away. Estimated time for the entire forest ecosystem to recover to the pre-1980 levels is about 200 years.
- Mount St. Helens is still an active volcano and it is fairly certain that it will erupt again in the future. It is closely monitored by scientists.

Within a couple of days Kade and the team had memorized most of these numbers, but kept the cards handy just in case they needed to refer to them.

The team jumped right into their work and Kade could tell they were all really enjoying this part of their detail. It was work, for sure, but it was also fun and educational; and more interesting than most of his fire details, Kade thought.

The rest of the day Wednesday and all day Thursday, the team alternated among the various work stations. They also sat in on as many of the theater programs as time allowed. They wanted to learn as much as they could before the heavy-use four-day period that would begin on Friday.

Rusty sat in on the presentation that one of the regular employees gave about Sasquatch. And was he ever excited!

"She said that many of the local residents still think there are Bigfoots around here," Elliott told Kade. "She even said that there were some recent reports of a sighting over near where we're staying in Castle Rock. Maybe we'll get to see Bigfoot some evening," Rusty said.

"Maybe," said Kade. "But I wouldn't get your hopes too high."

"Also," Elliott continued, "the lady showed a slide of that Bigfoot statue over in Toutle. Let's go over and see that some evening after work."

"We'll plan on it, Rusty," Kade promised. "And be sure to take plenty of photos."

"Definitely," said Rusty. "I want you to get one of me standing beside the statue."

Kade sat in on the Harry Truman presentation both Wednesday and Thursday. The more he learned about Ol' Harry, the more he wanted to know about this fellow native West Virginian. What a character!

On Thursday Kade had gathered all the handouts and information he could find in the Visitor Center about Truman. He also bought a book in the Visitor Center. It was titled, 'The Legend of Harry Truman – The Man and the Mountain He Loved.' Kade read through the material in any spare time he had on Thursday and Friday, as well as both evenings in his hotel room. By the time the weekend rolled around, Kade would come to know as much about Harry Truman as any of the regular employees of the Visitor center.

While Kade was intrigued by the Harry Truman story, he certainly didn't want to minimize the tragedy of the other 57 deaths caused by the eruption of Mount St. Helens. In particular, the death of U.S. Geological Survey (USGS) scientist David Johnston was a well-known and unfortunate legacy of the blast.

Johnston, a 30-year old volcanologist with USGS, was a principal scientist with the team that had been monitoring the volcano from an observation post six miles away from the mountain. He was on-site near the USGS trailer that day and was the first to report the eruption of May 18, 1980. He transmitted "Vancouver! Vancouver! This is it!" before being swept away by a lateral blast. Despite a thorough search, Johnston's body was never found.

Johnston had studied several volcanoes in North America and was considered an excellent and talented scientist. He thought that scientists must do whatever is necessary, including taking risks, to help protect the public from natural disasters. His work, and that of fellow USGS scientists, had convinced authorities to close Mount St. Helens to the public prior to the 1980 eruption. They maintained the closure despite heavy pressure to re-open the area; their work probably saved thousands of lives. Johnston's story was intertwined with the popular image of volcanic eruptions and their threat to society and it has become a part of volcano history.

By Friday the team felt well prepared to assist with duties at the Visitor Center and, as expected, the number of visitors increased substantially over the previous two days. And the next three days were likely to be even busier.

Kade had sat in on one more Harry Truman presentation in the theater on Friday and afterward told Mary Frances Evans that he would like to give the presentation himself the next few days. She enthusiastically agreed.

Jane, Lexi, and Gary had also learned the intricacies of running the audio-visual equipment and by this time they were starting, stopping, and re-setting the projectors and getting them ready for the next time slot.

Rusty was leading hikes on his own along Silver Lake and, with his enthusiastic style, had become quite a hit with the visitors. All of the team members were really enjoying themselves and felt good about the help they were providing to the regular staff.

After work on Friday, Rusty suggested they eat at a restaurant over toward Toutle before heading back to the motel. Kade knew that more than anything else, Rusty wanted to see the statue of Sasquatch in Toutle. It was just a drive of a few minutes and before long there it was for all the team to see – in the parking lot stood a 20-foot tall statue of Bigfoot.

"Finally," said Elliott. "This is what we all came to see."

"Really?" asked Comey. "All of us, or just you?"

"It's not like it's real or anything," commented Sustakis. "It's only a man-made statue."

"Yeah, but maybe they made it from a likeness of a real Sasquatch that someone saw around here," countered Elliot.

"Well," said Anderson, "based on the information I've read, plus what we've heard from the presentations at the Visitor Center, all reported sightings of Bigfoot claim that it is eight or nine feet tall, at the most."

"That's true. Not much taller than you, Rusty, " said Kade, smiling.

"Funny, funny guys," said Elliott. "All of you know darn well I'm only about 6' 3" and I sure don't weigh 300 or 400 pounds."

"Close though," said Comey with a big laugh.

"Let's stop all the small talk and get some photos before it gets too dark," said Elliott.

With that, the team all grabbed their cameras and each person took a few photos of the statue and of each other standing beside the Bigfoot. They asked one of the customers at the store to take a photo of the entire team standing beside the statue with each one of their cameras. Kade had also borrowed an instamatic camera from the Visitor Center and took a couple of "instant" shots of Rusty standing beside "his" Sasquatch.

"These are great," said Rusty, as the instant photos developed. "Thanks Kade."

"Which one is Rusty?" asked Comey.

"I think he's on the left," said Lexi.

"No, that's Bigfoot," said Jane. "I think Rusty is on the right, but I'm not sure."

"Well, they may not be brothers," laughed Kade, "but there is a strong resemblance."

"Definitely related," added Gary. "No doubt about it."

Elliott took the ribbing in good fun and he held on closely to the two photos that Kade gave him, as they walked across the parking lot to the restaurant. After dinner and the short drive back to The Sasquatch Inn, they all turned in early to rest before the next three busy days at the Visitor Center.

On Saturday Mary Frances Evans was able to schedule five of her experienced employees to work. With the five from back East, she would have ten staff members on duty – more than she had been able to schedule for any weekend the whole year. And it was a good thing. The visitor numbers for Saturday doubled from the previous day, which had been heavier than normal for a Friday.

Mary Frances would work today and tomorrow before taking a much needed two-day break herself on Monday and Tuesday. She and Kade had talked and decided that if the 'Easterners' could stay and work through

Wednesday, it would give her time to schedule rest days for her normal staff.

Kade's crew could drive to Vancouver Thursday morning, meet with Ron Perez for a debriefing, work on the draft of their report, and fly back home on Friday. That would mean Kade's crew would have worked an 18-day detail. He would alternate some rest time for Rusty, Jane, Lexi, Gary, and himself on Monday, Tuesday, and Wednesday. Kade checked and his crew members were all fine with that schedule.

Though they were all tired, they were having a blast. It was an important job they were doing and they all felt like they were contributing to one of the Forest Service's most important missions...serving people by being "good hosts."

Mary Frances said she would call Ron Perez at home that day to confirm the schedule which she and Kade had discussed and to make sure he was okay with this plan. If so, then Kade's crew would be in the Supervisor's Office next Thursday morning to meet with him around 10:00 a.m. They would check out of The Sasquatch Inn on Thursday morning, so Ron would need to make motel arrangements for Kade's crew in Vancouver for Thursday night, as well as make flight arrangements home for all five of the detailers. Evans told Kade that she should be able to get this all confirmed before she left work on Sunday evening.

Although it was non-stop all day for all ten of the Forest Service employees, Kade managed to slip off a couple of times to go over the note cards he had prepared for his presentation at 1:35 p.m. Yes, he was going to give the Harry Truman presentation himself today. And if it went well, he would handle it a few more times before they left to return home. He was a little nervous, but he also felt like he had all the information he needed to do a good job.

Kade had sat in on the Truman presentations in the Visitor Center theater on Wednesday, Thursday, and Friday. He also had read through all of the information he had accumulated about the man. He studied the pamphlets, booklets, and articles about "the man and his mountain" thoroughly on Thursday and Friday nights in the motel, too.

Kade wasn't going to glorify the man and his actions. After all, it was kind of irrational what Harry had done. But on the other hand, Truman was certainly a "character" and his saga was a colorful story intertwined with the Mount St. Helens event of May 18, 1980. Harry Truman did indeed love that mountain and that lake. He probably wouldn't have been one bit happy if he had lived, after the eruption of the volcano destroyed his lake. That was how Kade would present the story.

Kade grabbed an early lunch and shortly after the scheduled 1:05 p.m. slide show was done, he slipped into the theater for a few quiet moments before his presentation.

Here are some of the things Kade had learned about Harry Truman, which he hoped to cover during his talk:

- Harry Truman, like Kade, was a West Virginia native. Truman was born near the small community of Ivydale in Clay County, West Virginia in 1896.
- Harry's father, Newberry, was a logger, who loved to hunt, fish, and camp. Harry's mother, Rosa, served as the cook in the logging camps where Newberry was a foreman.
- Harry, his parents, and a younger sister all moved to the state of Washington, near the small town of Chehalis, in 1907, where Newberry continued to work in the logging business. Chehalis is just over an hour from Mount St. Helens.
- Harry was very mechanically oriented and had one of the first cars in the area when he was 17. It wouldn't run when his dad bought it, but Harry got it running and he became a hit with all of his friends. Prior to that, the Truman's had traveled by horse and buggy.

- Both Harry and his dad loved and made moonshine, dating from Newberry's days in West Virginia.
- Harry enlisted in the Army in World War I and his mechanical abilities were put to good use maintaining airplanes. He was on board the ship *Tuscania* off the coast of Ireland in 1918 and survived it being torpedoed. The *Tuscania* was transporting American troops to Europe when it was sunk by a German U-Boat, killing 210 of the 2,000-plus passengers and crew. The survivors were rescued by British Royal Navy Destroyers which were sailing in the area.
- Newberry was killed in a logging accident in 1923 and it wasn't long before Harry and two of his friends got involved in bootlegging and rum running of illegal alcohol.
- Harry never got caught and soon opened a garage in Chehalis, where he became well known for his mechanical touch with vehicles. He also began to search for supposed "lost" gold mines that he had heard about in the area near Spirit Lake. Harry continued the search off and on for several years with no luck.
- At one point Harry moved to Nevada to prospect for gold, but having no luck after several months, returned to Washington.
- All during these early years of Harry's life, he continued to make and sell moonshine. It had

been a Truman tradition since their West Virginia days. Harry made some pretty good money and he still never got caught.

- In 1928 Harry purchased the run down lodge at Spirit Lake. Over the next 10 years he gradually re-built it and added more cabins, other buildings, and he bought a few boats.
- Rumor has it that Harry and a friend did eventually find a lost pack train loaded with $20 gold pieces, which he hid and then used whenever he needed money for the lodge.
- Harry had lived, for the most part, at the Spirit Lake Lodge for nearly 53 years when Mount St. Helens erupted. He was 83 years old at the time of his death.
- His 16 cats and numerous "pet" raccoons were presumed to have perished along with Truman.
- Although Harry Truman was a well-known character in southwest Washington, he really wasn't known nationally until the months preceding the eruption of Mount St. Helens, when he gave colorful interviews and refused orders to leave the mountain.
- Due to national media coverage of his story, he received numerous letters from school kids across the country who were worried about his safety. Harry said he even received six marriage proposals. Harry had been married three times.

- Harry was a born story-teller and the notoriety of Mount St. Helens gave him ample audiences to spin his many tall tales. He seemed to relish his time in the national spotlight.
- Of the several celebrities said to have stayed at the Spirit Lake Lodge over the years, the one who became a close friend with Harry was Supreme Court Justice William Douglas. On Douglas' first visit, Truman didn't like him and was going to refuse to rent him a cabin. Once Harry found out who he was, he relented. They made up and became fast friends. Douglas visited Spirit Lake additional times, and Harry is reported to have visited Douglas in Washington, D.C.
- Several songs and poems were written about Harry Truman and Mount St. Helens. Also, there was a Mount St. Helens movie made, starring Art Carney as Harry Truman.

Kade's presentation went off without a hitch. The audience clapped at the end of the talk. They asked just a few questions and Kade was able to answer those. He didn't know it at the time, but Mary Frances Evans had slipped in and sat at the back during the presentation. She later told Kade that he had done an excellent job and that he was welcome to come back and give the presentation about Harry Truman any time.

Saturday was busy for the entire Forest Service crew and they were all glad when the day ended. It was back to the motel to eat, get a good night's sleep, and be ready for another busy day at the Visitor Center on Sunday.

Just before his alarm rang on Sunday morning, Kade was awakened by dogs barking out back of the motel. He figured he might as well get up anyway. As the dogs continued to bark, Kade looked through the back window and noticed a large shadowy figure running along the edge of the woods. Crazy joggers, Kade thought to himself. Who gets up to run this early in the morning?

At breakfast before heading to the Visitor Center, Gary said that dogs barking had awakened him earlier that morning. Kade mentioned that he had heard the dogs, too, and had seen a jogger or someone out back.

"Maybe it was Rusty," said Lexi. "He jogs most mornings before we eat."

"Not this morning," said Rusty. "I was really tired last night and slept in a little later this morning. And I never heard any dogs barking. Hey, maybe it was Bigfoot," said Rusty. "The motel manager said they've seen Bigfoots over in this area before."

"I don't think so," said Kade. "Although the jogger or whoever I saw did seem to be pretty big; maybe about Rusty's size."

"Well, it wasn't me," said Elliott. And the matter was dropped.

Sunday at the Visitor Center started fast. People were waiting at the door when they opened. And it never stopped all day – busy, busy, busy. But it made the day go faster for everyone. Kade gave another Harry Truman presentation and Jane Anderson told everyone that she felt like she could do a presentation Monday and Tuesday about the animals that were native to the area, as well as the migratory waterfowl. Mary Frances was agreeable and Jane was scheduled for presentations Monday morning and Tuesday afternoon.

Jane had initially studied wildlife management in college before finally settling on a degree in recreation management with an emphasis on outdoor interpretive work. She was well versed in the major mammals of North America and she was pretty much an expert when it came to waterfowl. Kade knew she would do a good job with her presentations.

One completely unexpected, but pleasant, surprise occurred just before lunch on Sunday. Kade had just finished walking around the exhibit hall, talking with visitors, when he heard someone near the front door yell, "Hey Kade; is that you Kade Holley?"

Turning around, Kade saw that a large group of visitors had just arrived; probably a bus tour or something, he thought. And pushing up through the crowd and heading toward Kade was a familiar face – a friend from back in Ohio. It was Roger Mulkey, a forester who worked for the Ohio Division of Forestry (ODOF). And right behind him was his wife Kerry, who was also a forester with the ODOF.

The Mulkeys were stationed at an ODOF office in northeastern Ohio. Kade had gotten to know them over the years from forestry meetings in Ohio and by serving with them on various statewide forestry committees. They had also taught together twice at a summer camp for junior and senior high school students interested in becoming foresters.

"What are you doing out here, Kade?" Roger asked. "Are you working? Did you get transferred out west? When I saw you at the state forestry meeting in June, you never said anything about taking a job in Washington," Roger went on.

"Whoa, Roger, slow down," said Kade. "I still work in Ohio. I'm just out here on a temporary assignment, with a group of Forest Service employees from back east. We're helping out during a time when they have been short-handed. I kind of volunteered, I think," Kade laughed. "Actually, I was getting ready to go west with a fire crew, when this assignment came up. So, here I am."

"But what about you?" Kade asked. "Are you driving a tour bus now?" smiled Kade.

"No," laughed Roger. "Actually, Kerry and I are on vacation. We flew into Seattle and are taking a seven-day bus tour ending up in San Francisco before we fly back to Ohio. This was one of our scheduled stops."

"It's a trip we've wanted to take and it's our 10th wedding anniversary," said Kerry. "It's been great so far, and what a surprise to see one of our "Ohio Buckeyes" working here at the Mount St. Helens Visitor Center."

"Well, I'm enjoying this assignment, but I am getting a little homesick," said Kade. "This coming Tuesday will make two weeks from the day we flew out here. But we should be finished with everything by Thursday and fly back home on Friday. Hey, I don't know how long your tour bus will be here, but at 1:35 p.m. I give a presentation in the theater on Harry Truman. Maybe you can sit in on that," Kade said.

"The tour leader said we should all meet back at the bus at 2:00 p.m.," said Kerry. "So, I think we can listen to your presentation."

"Isn't Harry Truman the old guy who refused to leave the mountain before it blew up?" asked Roger. "I remember reading about him several years ago."

"That's him," said Kade. "It's an interesting story, that's for sure. And come to find out, he was born in West Virginia, like I was."

"All of you West Virginians are stubborn old coots, aren't you?" laughed Roger. "We'll be at your presentation. Oh, by the way," Roger added. "There's another guy and his wife on this tour from Ohio. I didn't know him before the trip, but he works for the Soil Conservation Service (SCS) down your way, in the southern part of the state. You might have run into him. His name is J.C. Cameron," said Roger.

"J.C. Cameron!" Kade said excitedly. "I know him well. He's a District Conservationist in the same county I'm located in. What a coincidence. It sure is a small world. Be sure to tell him to look me up before your bus leaves."

"Will do," said Roger. "I guess we'd better look around the Visitor Center now. Your presentation starts in just over an hour. See you then."

Kade and Cameron were able to connect a little while later and each one was amazed about the coincidence of them meeting 2,500 miles away from their normal work locations. J.C. said that he and his wife would take in Kade's presentation about Harry Truman, too.

The theater was packed for Kade's presentation, but he was well prepared and not the least bit nervous. He took a minute at the beginning to introduce himself and tell the audience where he was from, in addition to recognizing his friends from Ohio. Afterward he told Roger and Kerry that he would see them at the Winter Ohio Forestry meeting in Columbus and he told J.C. that he would stop by the SCS office to visit when he got back home.

The rest of the day was busy, but things went well for both the visitors and the staff. Mary Frances reminded Kade that she would be off the next two days, Monday and Tuesday, and that she would also schedule half of her workers off the same two days. The other half of her normal staff would be off Tuesday and Wednesday. That meant that Kade's five-person team would staff the Visitors Center by themselves on Tuesday. Kade and his team were confident they could handle duties on that day, which should be quite a bit slower than things had been these past couple of days.

Monday was Labor Day and fairly busy, though not nearly like Saturday and Sunday had been. Ron Perez called in the afternoon and told Kade that he would stop by on Tuesday to make sure things were going okay since the team would be working there alone. He also confirmed the schedule that Mary Frances and Kade had agreed to and said that he would have the exit meeting with Kade's crew on Thursday morning in the Supervisor's Office.

Jane's wildlife and waterfowl presentation went really well and afterward many of the visitors took the trail walk with Rusty. They were pleased to see four different species of waterfowl on the hike along Silver Lake.

By Tuesday the team was performing like old pros. Though the visitor usage was down somewhat, they were busy all day since they had no regular Gifford Pinchot National Forest personnel to help them. This made the team appreciate the job the regular Visitor Center staff had done over the past several weeks when so many of their fellow workers had been away on fire details.

Kade and Jane gave their presentations once again and Ron Perez stopped by to see how things were going. He was very appreciative of the help that Kade's team had been providing at the Visitor Center. He shared that Mary Frances couldn't believe how quickly the team had learned their "new" duties and how well they were doing. She wanted them to stay longer, but Ron explained that about two weeks on this assignment was all that had been agreed upon by the Regional Foresters in Portland and Milwaukee.

Ron gave Kade the information for their motel in Vancouver. He also told Kade that he would have their plane reservations and tickets available for them at their exit meeting in the Supervisor's Office on Thursday.

Wednesday came and Mary Frances was back with some of her regular staff. Kade's team was glad of that on one hand, but each one of them was also a little sad that this special assignment was nearing its end. It had been hard work and great fun at the same time.

At the end of the day, goodbye's and thank you's were shared by all. Mary Frances presented each of the team members with a coffee cup that had "Mount St. Helens Visitor Center" printed on one side and "Gifford Pinchot National Forest" on the other.

At dinner that evening the team talked about their past two weeks and they each felt like the experience had been productive and worthwhile. Everyone had learned a lot, as well as sharing their talents and insights with the Gifford Pinchot National Forest personnel. The final report would include numerous commendations as well as some recommendations from the team.

Near the end of the meal, Rusty said, "Hey, why don't we stay up all night and try to see the Bigfoot that roams out back of the motel?"

"Not me," Lexi and Jane said almost simultaneously.

"Me neither," replied Gary. "I'm tired and need a good night's sleep. I don't believe there's such a thing as Bigfoot anyway."

"Oh yes there is," said Rusty. "Didn't you read the brochures and information at the Visitor Center?"

"That's just an old folk tale," said Gary. "If there are Bigfoots, then how come no one has ever found a real one – dead or alive?"

"It's because they're so elusive," Rusty explained. "If I worked out here, you can bet that I'd probably be the first person to ever prove that they're real. Kade, you believe that there really are Bigfoots, don't you?"

"Not sure, Rusty," Kade answered. "But if you believe there are Bigfoots, then that is fine with me. But I wouldn't go roaming around out back, just in case. If there is one out there, it might think you're an enemy or something and try to hurt you."

"No," Comey laughed. "It would probably think Rusty was a cousin or long-lost little brother and take him back to see the king or ruler of the clan, or whatever they call the main Bigfoot."

"Well, Gary, if a Bigfoot caught you, it would probably think you were just a little animal cracker and eat you in one bite," Rusty countered.

"That sounds like enough, guys," said Kade. "Let's turn in and get some rest. We have to check out in the morning after breakfast and be in Vancouver for that 10:00 a.m. meeting."

"And don't let the Bigfoots bite, or I mean, don't let the bed bugs bite," laughed Jane.

Rusty didn't laugh.

On Thursday morning the team ate breakfast, checked out of The Sasquatch Inn, and got on the road to Vancouver. None of the team, including Rusty, had stayed up very late the night before. They were all starting to feel the effects of their long assignment. Rusty said he had thought about setting the alarm for 2:00 or 3:00 in the morning to get up and try to see Bigfoot, but told the team he was so tired he decided not to.

"Just as well," said Comey. "They don't exist, anyway."

"I'm pretty sure they do," replied Rusty. "You're just afraid of them and wouldn't know what to do if you did see one."

"Yes, I know what I'd do," Comey laughed. "I'd try my best to wake up from the dream I was having."

"Hey, Rusty," said Lexi. "Ever try to stay up when you were younger to try and see Santa Claus or the Tooth Fairy?"

"Maybe," said Rusty. "What's it to you anyway?"

"I was just wondering how that turned out," Lexi smiled.

"I'm sure gonna miss being part of this team," remarked Jane.

"Me, too," said Kade.

By the time the team arrived in Vancouver, located the Supervisor's Office, checked in at the front desk, and found the conference room, it was a few minutes before the meeting with Ron Perez was to begin.

"Hello everyone," said Perez, entering the conference room. "Good to see all of you. I can't believe it's time for you to return home. It sure has gone fast. We certainly appreciate all that you've done for us. And we look forward to receiving your final report. How did your final night go in Castle Rock? Hope you had a good night's rest."

"Well, we almost had a Bigfoot abduction," replied Comey, as Jane and Lexi giggled. "It was quite tense there for a while. Other than that, we all slept well."

"Seems like your group has bonded and had a lot of fun together," Perez said to Kade.

"I think so," said Kade. "They do like to kid one another, that's for certain. But they all worked hard and we have enjoyed our time here."

Ron then explained what he would like to have covered in the final report. It matched up pretty well with what Kade had in mind, too. Ron said they could spend the rest of the day in the conference room working on the draft before heading to their motel. He gave Kade the information and directions to the motel.

He also gave each team member the paperwork needed for their return flights back home on Friday. They were to leave the Forest Service van in the motel parking lot and take a shuttle over to the airport. Ron and another employee would drive over and pick up the van Friday morning.

"If there are no questions," Ron said, "I'd like to leave each of you with some tokens of our appreciation from the Gifford Pinchot National Forest. First, we have a framed Certificate of Appreciation for each of you."

The certificates were signed by both the Forest Supervisor and the Mount St. Helens Monument Manager and read "Thank you for sharing your time and talents with the visitors and staff of the Gifford Pinchot National Forest and the Mount St. Helens Visitor Center." All the words were printed over a light background photo of the eruption of the volcano.

"We also normally give a coffee mug to special guests," Ron continued, "but Mary Frances told me she was going to give you each a mug from the Visitor Center. So, I talked with Kade about sizes and we came up with something we hope you will wear with pride."

Ron then presented each team member with a polo shirt with the Gifford Pinchot National Forest logo above the left breast and their name embroidered opposite on the right side. They were all very pleased with the gift and thanked Ron, several times each.

"Oh yes, there's one more thing," Perez said. "For Rusty, we have a special cap."

Ron then pulled out a ball cap which had a likeness of a

Sasquatch printed on it with the words "Bigfoot Country – Castle Rock, WA."

"Cool," said Rusty. "I almost bought one of these the other day anyway. Thank you very much. I'll accept this from one Bigfoot believer to another," Rusty said.

The team said its goodbye's to Ron Perez and then began pulling together notes from the past week to start on a draft of their report.

"Don't forget, Kade," Rusty said later that afternoon, "you promised to mention Bigfoot or Sasquatch in the final report. Remember?"

"We'll see," replied Kade. "But I don't remember promising anything like that for sure."

The team finished its work and headed to their motel. They decided to have an early dinner and say their goodbye's that evening because their flights all left at different times Friday morning. After dinner, Kade told everyone how much he appreciated their hard work and dedication over the past two weeks. He said it was absolutely the best group he had ever worked with on a special assignment.

Kade had all the write-up materials with him and he promised that he would have a final draft for them to review within a week to ten days. If he needed any further information, as he worked on the final, he would call them next week. Kade noticed that Rusty was proudly wearing his Bigfoot cap.

"And if you need any information about Bigfoot for the report, you can call me anytime," said Rusty. The other team members smiled and Kade said he'd be sure to do that.

After handshakes and hugs, they each went back to their rooms and got ready for their flights home the next day.

****

As Kade had promised the team, and despite a heavy workload back home in getting caught up after being gone for 2 ½ weeks, he had a final draft report ready for them to review early the second week after his return. He had called each member, including Gary Comey twice, to clarify some of the information. He also had a "surprise" for Rusty Elliott in the report.

Among Kade's many duties as District Ranger, he had been writing a weekly column for the local newspaper for the past three years. It was intended to keep local citizens informed about activities on the national forest; clear up any rumors that circulated from time to time; feature human interest stories about Forest Service employees and local residents involved in natural resource activities; and provide general informational columns about forestry and the outdoors.

It was a great way to connect with people and get them to know the Forest Service better. He had received many positive comments from folks around town about the various columns he had written. When Kade was away on assignment or on vacation, other District employees took turns writing the column for him. He wanted it to appear weekly and not just from time to time.

The first week he was back at work, Kade had written a column giving an overview about the assignment to the Gifford Pinchot National Forest and Mount St. Helens. In the future he would write a column specifically about the Visitor Center work they did, the Harry Truman story, and mention the chance meeting in the state of Washington with J.C. Cameron, as well as Roger and Kerry Mulkey.

Kade had already written a second column after his return home. He knew that Gary Comey, Lexi Sustakis, and Jane Anderson would enjoy it, and he sincerely hoped that Rusty Elliott would, too. It was his "surprise" for Rusty - an inclusion about Bigfoot in the final report.

Here is that column:

"As mentioned in this column last week, I worked in Bigfoot country for a couple of weeks last month on the Gifford Pinchot National Forest in Washington. That legend is intact in the Mount St. Helens area because everywhere you went it was Bigfoot this, or Sasquatch that.

There were many pictures and paintings and souvenirs and so on. And near the town of Toutle stood a large statue-like Bigfoot, about 20 feet tall. At least I think it was a statue; either that or an amazingly still and quiet, large ape.

I came across a note recently telling about four sets of footprints found last Spring in the Blue Mountains, just a few hours east of where I worked. An anthropologist from Washington State University said that the prints appear to be authentic and made by an ape-like animal, perhaps as large as eight feet high and weighing 800 pounds or so.

According to the article, the thing that separates these prints from earlier ones (some of which were definite fakes) is that the dermal ridges are clearly shown. Dermal ridges are similar to fingerprints and according to the anthropologist, they cannot be faked. About 40 experts have examined the prints and most of them believe the prints are authentic.

The story went on to tell about some film footage taken of a female Sasquatch. It was examined by Disney Studios, which said that the only people who could have faked something that realistic was the Disney Studio itself -- and they indicated that they had not done it.

So who knows? Maybe I was out there in the boonies of Washington, right beside a Bigfoot or two. Lucky for me they're supposed to be shy and docile creatures.

As I think back on it, there was one morning out there when I arose early and happened to notice a large, shadowy figure out back of the motel where we were staying, right on the edge of the woods. I thought at the time it was probably Rusty Elliott out for an early morning jog or something.

Rusty, from Vermont's Green Mountain National Forest, was with us on the trip and he loosely fits the Sasquatch description -- large, hairy, and big feet. (apologies, Rusty, but it's true).

I'm gonna give ol' Rusty a call and see if he did indeed jog on some of those mornings. If he didn't, then I, too, might become a member of

the BBC -- Bigfoot Believers Club. I'll keep you posted."

Kade included both of his recent newspaper columns in the addendum to the team's final report. He also explained in a short lead-in paragraph what the columns were and the fact that the second one was somewhat "tongue-in-cheek."

Lexi, Gary, and Jane each called Kade after reading the draft report and said they were glad that he had included the addendum about Bigfoot. Kade worried that Rusty was upset.

But a few days later Kade received a note in the mail from Rusty who said that the report looked fine to him; he wouldn't change a thing, not even the part about Bigfoot. Relieved, Kade made a few changes to the draft that were suggested by the other three team members and then fired off the final report to Ron Perez.

The team had some suggestions about campgrounds, hiking trails, parking areas, and observation points. They made a number of recommendations about the hiking trail up to the volcano rim, permits, limits on numbers of hikers, and rest facilities. There was a section suggesting more signs in certain locations, as well as additional information that should go on bulletin boards, and landscaping ideas for specific sites. There were a few recommendations for the Visitor Center itself; not many, because that seemed to be a first-class operation.

The team had included a generous "commendation" section in the final report. There were a lot of great things happening on the Gifford Pinchot National Forest and the Mount St. Helens National Volcanic Monument, in particular. Plus, Kade had included a page thanking everyone out there for the opportunity to participate in this project. He gave special thanks to Ron Perez, Kent Dorman, Don Mastick, and Mary Frances Evans – all of whom had made them feel welcome and useful. Their planning and attention to detail had made this assignment a pleasure.

As Kade reflected back on the Mount St. Helens assignment, he was reminded how fortunate he was to work for the U.S. Forest Service and to have those kinds of opportunities. There was always something new and always something exciting happening when you were a "ranger" for the Forest Service.

EXHIBIT

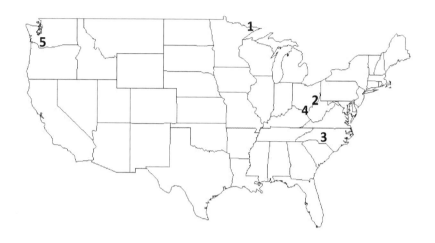

1. Superior National Forest – Ely, Minnesota

2. Wayne National Forest – Marietta, Ohio

3. Uwharrie National Forest – Troy, North Carolina

4. Wayne National Forest – Ironton, Ohio

5. Gifford Pinchot National Forest – Mount St. Helens, Washington

REFERENCES

1) Various USDA Forest Service websites, including the site for the Gifford Pinchot National Forest.

2) *The Legend of Harry Truman*, Editor, Mary Ann Woosley; copyright 1981 by C.F. Boone Publishers, Inc.

3) *Eruptions of Mount St. Helens: Past, Present, and Future* by Robert I. Tilling, USDI/U.S. Geological Survey, 1990.

POSTSCRIPT

I sincerely hope you have enjoyed this first series of stories in the adventures of Kade Holley, Forest Ranger. In this first book Kade's career as a Forester with the U.S. Forest Service took him to National Forests in Minnesota, Ohio, North Carolina, and Washington. Future stories will include assignments in West Virginia, Georgia, Kentucky, Colorado, and other states, as well as more adventures in the states from the first book. Kade's formative years as a young boy, which led him to pursue a forestry career, will be covered. In addition, there will be adventures such as:

- Searching for lost hunters in the mountains of West Virginia;
- Dealing with black bears in the north Georgia mountains;
- More stories on forest fires;
- A smelly encounter with buzzards;
- A moose adventure in Minnesota;
- Canoe mishaps and helicopter flights;
- And a Colorado assignment that included a ride in a Grand Prix race car driven by future Indianapolis 500 Champion, Scott Dixon.

Yes, Kade Holley's life is never dull. But as Kade has said many times, "That's life as a Forest Ranger with the U.S. Forest Service; and I love it."

I hope you will join me by reading future books about **Kade Holley, Forest Ranger.**

OTHER BOOKS BY DAN KINCAID

The Penicillin Kids, the 1966 West Virginia Class AA State Basketball Champions, copyright 2015.

Your.....Wayne National Forest, a historical collection of the author's weekly Ohio newspaper columns from 1981 and 1982, copyright 2016.

Your.....Chattahoochee National Forest, a historical collection of the author's weekly Georgia newspaper columns from December 1978 – June 1980, copyright 2016.

All three books are available on Amazon.com.

AUTHOR BIO

Dan Kincaid's **Kade Holley** stories are works of fiction, although they have their roots in his 31-year career with the U.S. Forest Service. Kincaid worked at national forest locations in West Virginia, Ohio, Minnesota, Georgia, and North Carolina, as well as temporary details, training and various other assignments in Colorado, Kentucky, California, Indiana, Washington, Montana, and Tennessee. He also spent several years with the Forest Service's State & Private Forestry branch. After retirement in his final position as a District Ranger, Kincaid worked another six years for state forestry agencies in West Virginia and Ohio and two years as a contractor for the Wayne National Forest in Ohio. Earlier in his career he spent 2 ½ years in Public Affairs with Westvaco Corporation, a leading manufacturer of paper products.

Kincaid received a Bachelor of Science degree in Forest Resource Management from West Virginia University, a Masters degree in Forestry/Environmental Management from Duke University, and a Teaching Certification for Biology and General Science, Grades 7-12, from Marietta College in Ohio.

From 1978 to 1990 Kincaid wrote a weekly newspaper column about forestry and the Forest Service for various newspapers in Ohio and Georgia. In addition, for 5 ½ years (1985-90), he wrote a separate weekly hunting/fishing column for The Marietta Times daily newspaper in Ohio and served as a sportswriter/ columnist for games, events and activities in a two-state, multi-county area. He has had over 1,000 columns and stories published under his by-line. Kincaid also served as a Public Information Officer for both federal and state agencies; a Fire Information and Public Information Officer on various fires and other incidents; has given numerous presentations to natural resource professionals on public relations and the media; and written hundreds of news releases, ads, speeches, texts for pamphlets/brochures, and other related items.

69202399R00109

Made in the USA
San Bernardino, CA
12 February 2018